SILENT
MOUNTAIN

SILENT MOUNTAIN

TENTH ANNIVERSARY EDITION
- 2023 -

Published by
Candy Jar Books
Mackintosh House
136 Newport Road
Cardiff, CF24 3LT
www.candyjarbooks.co.uk

ISBN: 978-0-9571548-1-0

Cover by Steve Upham
Illustrations by Terry Cooper

Printed and bound in the UK
4edge, 22 Eldon Way, Hockley, Essex, SS5 4AD

For Andy, Jacob and Nieve

Chapter One

Jack knew he could outrun the bullies. He was the fastest boy in his school year, but he was running in the wrong direction. He needed to lead them away from his home. He veered left on Alpine Lane and raced towards the park. Looking over his shoulder he noticed that they were getting slower. Quickly he sprinted down the hill. Ahead of him was a bandstand. He dived behind the green painted boards and crouched down very low, waiting for his breath to return. With any luck they would turn around and go home. He checked to see if the book was still in his pocket. His precious book, still wrapped in its plastic cover. Safe!

Kyle Johnson and George Stubbs were striding towards the bandstand, breathing heavily. As if Jack didn't have enough going on in his life – now the bullying had become physical.

'Don't they ever give up?' he whispered, feeling trapped and wishing he'd chosen to run through the streets instead.

He looked around but there was nowhere to hide. The lake lay silent and still in front of him, with the shrubs and trees all winter dead. There wasn't anywhere to go except the way he had come. Looking around desperately he noticed some splintered pieces of wood on the ground. With relief he realised that someone had pulled a plank away. He lay flat and shuffled himself through the gap underneath the bandstand stage. Just in time.

'He's here somewhere,' Johnson said, still trying to catch his breath and stepping up onto the octagonal platform.

'Nah, he's gone,' Stubbs panted, joining him. 'He must have turned and run up the Sanctuary when we couldn't see him. He's probably gone to fill in his stupid little book with some more facts about butterflies,' he said in a teasing, high-pitched voice.

Jack lay still among the old carrier bags, papers, bottles and litter that had collected under the bandstand. Stubbs lit a cigarette, dropping the match. It fell between the planks and landed just in front of Jack's nose, still alight. He blew at it quietly, suddenly seeing himself laying in the middle of a giant tinder box.

'Little freak!' Johnson wheezed nastily, his words echoing around the silent park. 'You should have seen his face when you slapped him. Your hand print was actually on his cheek!' They both laughed maliciously, sounding like two hyenas circling their prey.

'What about the look he gave me tho'? I thought for a minute he was going to fight me. Lucky he took off or he'd be under my size tens now,' Stubbs said, thumping his foot down hard.

Jack looked up. *If only they knew!*

'C'mon, it's freezin'. I ain't staying here all evening. We'll get him some other time,' Stubbs said loudly, still chuffing on his cigarette. 'Who does he think he is? Wait till next time and I'll set fire to his pathetic little book!'

'Yeah, maybe we could set fire to both of them,' Johnson

said hatefully.

They stepped down from the bandstand and began walking up the hill. Jack waited until he could no longer hear their voices. He shuffled out from his hiding place, pulled his knees up to his chest and began to cry.

'Oh, there you are, love. I was starting to worry. Where've you been?' asked Jack's mum, as she greeted him at his front door.

'Over Tim's. Xbox... you know...' he mumbled. Jack hated lying to his mum.

'I'm just going up to get changed,' he said as he slid past her trying not to make eye contact, and he ran upstairs to his room.

'All right then, I've got some tea on. Oh, Gran phoned. Can you pop over to see her tomorrow? I said you'd give her a call when you got in.'

His mum was already going back to the kitchen.

'Yeah, will do,' he replied sadly, wishing he could tell her what had happened today, but more importantly wishing he could tell his dad.

Chapter Two

Jack was standing at the side of the lake. He knew he shouldn't have come back and that his mum would be really angry with him. It hadn't snowed yet, but it was freezing. 'Snow cold,' his gran called it. It had that smell that you couldn't describe, but you knew it anyway. The smell that came just before mammoth, grey clouds unloaded their wintery contents onto trees, cars and roads.

His gran would be cross too. She really was spooky sometimes. She said she knew things about the future. She called it her *talent*. This always made Jack smile and perhaps he did actually believe some of what his gran said. Her prediction about him breaking his arm playing football had been spot on, and the time she'd said his little sister Joley was going to win some money was right too. Okay, it was a £5 book token, but she'd still been right. But then she hadn't foreseen the most important thing of all, the only thing he really wished she had.

But he was here now, wasn't he? If he didn't believe what she'd said, why had he come? His gran had made a prophecy just two hours earlier. They had been sitting in front of her coal fire drinking hot chocolate with little marshmallow floaters. The combined heat of the fire, and hot chocolate, and the familiar papery smell of old books

4

piled high in every corner had almost put him in a trance. As he watched the light from the jumping flames turn her silver-grey hair to warm amber, his gran had told him not to go to the lake. Something was going to happen there.

'When?' Jack had asked.

'Soon, very soon,' she had replied, smiling at him gently.

She didn't give him any details. She never did. Her troubled look said everything.

'Stay away from the lake,' she'd warned.

'I'm not going anywhere,' Jack had promised. 'It's way too cold.'

'*The freeze* is coming. You need to stay safe.'

This worried Jack, he only had to look outside to see that the freeze was already here. It was the depths of winter after all.

His gran was a wiry little woman of seventy-six. It looked like a strong wind might blow her over, but she was strong in a different way. She had suffered terribly during the Second World War when both her parents had been killed during bombing raids. Later in her life, Jack's grandad, his gran's husband, had died when Jack's dad had been a child, so she'd had to bring up his dad on her own. But despite all the sad things that had happened to her, she was big-hearted and great fun to be around. They always had a good chuckle together and his gran wasn't above being told the odd rude joke either. She would wheeze out a great big laugh and tears would roll down her face. He didn't want his gran to ever get like other people's grans – old!

Now he had broken his promise to her.

This was a test, he thought. *To see if his gran really was going a bit strange.*

But he wasn't quite sure what to look for. The parkland surrounding the lake, that was usually filled with kids after school and on weekends, was unnaturally deserted. No one was bold enough, or stupid enough, to brave the icy wind and freezing temperature. He walked carefully down to the edge of the lake. The muddy ground had hardened and was slippery with ice crystals that cracked under his feet. He looked across the still water. On the other side he could see the woodland, dense and dead in the grey, winter light.

Every summer he had come here with his dad and little sister, Joley. They had brought his bright yellow dinghy and the three of them had paddled across to the other side. It wasn't that far, but it had felt like a huge adventure: the three of them with their picnic, gliding across the water to their own private island. The woodland was really just a small copse. It was only a short walk through the trees to reach the main road that circled the village of Vale, where they lived. But it was still great fun to sit at the edge of the lake or play in the bushy, green woodland, or look for butterflies and bugs, and spot birds using his *Observer Book of Birds and Nature*.

On his tenth birthday Jack had sat at the breakfast table with his dad, Joley and his mum, opening his gifts. The little book had sat on the top, neatly wrapped in bright birthday paper.

'This is from me, just me,' his dad had said quietly to him. Jack had looked up and seen his mum raise her eyebrows and smile. His dad had always bought a 'just-from-me gift' for both him and his sister since they were old enough to remember. Jack had been delighted with the book if only for the reason that it would mean him and his dad would be going out together spotting birds on their weekends.

'I was given one of these when I was a child,' his dad had smiled. 'Take it with you everywhere. You never know when you might need to use it.'

While most kids Jack's age, twelve, were worshipping celebrities and footballers, he secretly admired Peter Finchborough, the famous naturalist who presented all his favourite nature programmes on TV. He carried his *Observer* book with him everywhere – and although he had tried not to let the kids at school see it – that was how he had found himself dead centre of Johnson and Stubbs' bully radar. The book had dropped out of his pocket and Stubbs had picked it up first, and thrown it to Johnson. They'd seen all his notes on the woodland birds and butterflies. He'd been lucky to snatch it back from them, but they hadn't left him alone about it since.

He knelt down by the side of the lake and peered into the murkiness. Everything, including the water, was grey at this time of year. It looked like all the colour had drained from the world, leaving just a black-and-white photograph behind. He removed one glove and dipped his fingertips into the bitterly cold water. As he did so, he heard the strangest sound. A crackling noise echoed across the expanse of water, sounding just like a huge branch breaking from an ancient tree.

Jack looked around him, searching for the source of the noise. With a start of surprise he realised the lake was beginning to ice over. He watched in amazement as the

freeze crept slowly outwards from the middle, just like small, thin, white fingers. He had never seen anything like this before, and was sure it was not a normal occurrence – even in winter. He was so mesmerised by the water freezing that he forgot that his fingers, now completely numb, were still immersed in the water at the edge of the lake. As he pulled his hand quickly away, something strong and cold beneath the surface caught him by the wrist. As much as he tried to scramble backwards he could not pull free. Jack was terrified and tried to scream, but his throat was tight with fear. He fell forward onto his stomach and hit the ice. With a deafening sound just like a whip being cracked, it gave way under his weight. His breath was taken away as he sank, deeper and deeper under the ice. He opened his eyes to see black webbed fingers wrapped tightly around his wrist. Desperately he looked for some way to escape, but in horror saw the split ice was closing above him. Jack was overwhelmed by the deepest sadness he had ever felt. Just like the day his dad had died.

Chapter Three

The sound of chattering teeth made Jack open his eyes. He was on his back looking up at the sky. It was the same hard, grey colour that it had been earlier. He had the feeling of not really being inside his own body, but then he became aware of himself as he realised the chattering teeth were his own!

What had happened?

His mind was quite clear. He remembered every detail right up until the time he thought he was going to die. But he had absolutely no idea how he was dead!

He sat up and began to shiver violently. His clothes were soaked through. His hat and scarf were gone and he'd also lost a glove and a welly. He looked across the lake, back to where he had been kneeling just moments ago.

Or was it hours? He didn't know how long it had been. He scooted backwards on his bottom, leaving a wet trail in the mud like a crocodile slide.

I've got to get moving, he thought. *I've got to get home or I'll die from the cold.*

He pushed himself up onto shaky legs and moved further back, his eyes not leaving the frozen water for a moment. His limbs felt heavy and painful. He had always been quite resourceful but, since his dad had gone, Jack had lost the confidence to make decisions. This time, though, he knew just what he had to do. He continued to walk backwards until he reached the edge of the woodland. Only then did he take his terrified eyes off the lake, release his breath, and turn around to face the leafless, naked trees. He knew the way through and began to jog. Jack knew he could make it to the road in twenty minutes at a steady pace, but the weight of his soaking clothes and the loss of his boot, not to mention his shivering body, made it impossible for him to move at any kind of speed.

He was beginning to fear that it would be dark before he got to the road. He had left his gran's house at about three o'clock and he didn't have any idea how long he'd been in the water. He touched his wrist to find his watch had gone. Suddenly he panicked as the memories of the black webbed fingers engulfed him. He began to run as fast as his clothes would allow him, praying that no one he knew would drive past as he hobbled along the road. His gran's house was the closest. He rang the bell and she opened the door. Her smile immediately dropped from her face when she saw him.

'Oh, my boy!' she cried. 'What on earth happened?'

She ushered him into her warm front room not waiting for a reply. The coal fire was still burning, welcoming him with its wonderful heat. Jack just stood and shivered. He was far too cold to speak.

'I've got some spare things of yours upstairs. I'll go and get them,' she said, hurrying out of the room.

She returned quickly with his clothes and handed him a fluffy white towel.

'I'll go and make some hot chocolate. Get out of those

clothes and dry yourself before you catch your death,' she ordered him.

Jack stripped and changed as soon as she left the room, dumping his clothes in a wet heap on the floor. She came back carrying two steaming mugs of chocolate.

'Right, my boy, I think you have some explaining to do,' his gran said sternly. She looked at him and waited.

'So... I sort of went to the lake... well to see... you know... you said the freeze was coming. I didn't really believe you.'

Jack couldn't get his words out and started to feel very guilty.

'Oh, Jack, you promised me. Did someone hurt you?' She sounded very disappointed in him. Jack realised that if she had asked this question yesterday he would have told her about Johnson and Stubbs, but that was a story for another day.

'Well, someone or something... I'm not sure. There was something in the lake, I don't know what it was, but one minute the lake was water and then suddenly it froze, right in front of me! It was so weird, Gran. Then this thing... it pulled me in... under the ice. I don't even know how I got out. I think I fainted.' Jack's voice quivered as he told the story. He saw a shadow cross his gran's face then she almost spilled her hot chocolate.

'Gran? What is it?' he asked apprehensively. She was very pale.

'What did you see, Jack? What pulled you into the lake? Do you mean other boys?'

'No, I mean... I didn't really see it... but it had these

12

webbed fingers... I think... I don't really know.'

'Webbed fingers? Are you sure?'

'Well... I was pulled into the lake... but the water was really murky.'

His gran looked at him as if seeing him for the first time.

'Oh dear, what have I done? Oh dear!' she suddenly cried out.

Jack was confused and worried now.

'Gran, what is it? What's going on? I don't understand. What do you mean, "what have *you* done?"'

'Jack, this is very important. You must listen to me. I will tell you everything, but not now... later... in the morning. I need some time to gather my thoughts. I have to think about this. I have made a terrible, terrible mistake and I must put it right. I *will* put it right, I promise you.' She was rambling now and Jack's concern turned to fear.

She continued, 'But you are not, I repeat NOT to go to the lake again! We will speak in the morning and I will explain everything. Do you understand me?'

His gran was looking straight into his eyes. Her face had the same look it had just after his dad had died.

'Why, Gran? What's happening there? Do you know? I don't think I imagined it...'

His gran ignored the questions. 'Promise me, Jack, or I will phone your mother and you can explain how you ended up in the lake to her.'

Jack knew this wasn't an idle threat. He didn't want to tell his mum anything about his afternoon. She would ground him forever if she knew that he had been to the lake, never mind that he had been drowning in it!

'Okay, I promise. But you have to promise me too, that you will tell me everything tomorrow.'

His gran smiled gently at him now. She had regained her composure.

'I will, I promise. Now go and phone your mum. Tell her you're having tea with me and staying over.'

Jack did as he was told, but he suddenly felt very weary. His head and body ached, and he needed to sleep. Once he'd rung his mum, he asked, 'Gran, is it okay if I go to bed now? I'll eat something later on. I'm really tired.'

His gran nodded. She was staring at the fire, lost in her thoughts. 'Your bed's made up,' she said absently.

Jack made his way up the narrow cottage stairs to his bedroom.

He woke much later to a quiet, sleeping house and a grumbling stomach. He had fallen asleep in his clothes and his gran had put a fleecy red blanket over him. He got up and went downstairs to the kitchen.

The clock on the cooker flashed 11.45pm. Jack was starving. Opening the fridge he found a pile of beef sandwiches wrapped in cling film. He pulled out the milk and helped himself to a large glass. While sitting and eating at the round kitchen table his mind raced through the events of the day. He was desperate to know what was going on. None of it seemed real to him.

Finishing his food, he was about to return to bed when a sudden panic overcame him.

My Observer book! Where is it?

He'd had it at the lake but...

Oh no, no, no!

He couldn't remember it being in his trouser pocket as he sat shivering on the bank. Those clothes were now in his gran's washing machine. He reached into the machine and pulled out his soggy trousers. There was nothing in the pockets, but his gran would have checked anyway. He raced to the front room hoping to find the book drying in the fading warmth of the fire. It wasn't there. Jack felt like crying. He thought about waking his gran, but he had seen how distracted she had been. He didn't want to wake her and frighten her again.

The only other place it could be was at the lake.

Maybe it was still there, somewhere. It might have slipped from his pocket when he was being dragged into the water. It was in its plastic cover. Perhaps it was still okay.

He had to go back to the lake, but that would mean he had to defy his gran and he hated the idea of doing that.

Still, if he went now he would be back in twenty minutes. His gran was asleep; she would never know he'd been out. He would take her key and return it to the hook by the front door when he got back. He didn't want to deceive her, but he hated to admit his need to find his book was more important.

He tiptoed quietly along the hallway, slipping on a pair of his old trainers from the shoe rack. He silently opened the front door, and glanced guiltily up the stairs before closing the door behind himself.

Chapter Four

Jack thought about the book as he jogged quickly back to the lake. Without it he had nothing left to connect him to his dad, his dad's handwriting was even on some of the pages. The idea of losing it hurt him far too much.

It was very dark. Jack had decided against going through the woodland. Some of his common sense still remained, though it didn't feel like he got closer to his destination He would check that side in daylight if he needed to. He walked down to the bank. The lake was still frozen and there was a silence unlike anything he had ever experienced. He almost expected a wolf to howl. Weak moonlight reflected off the cold, solid surface, but it was not a clear night. Night clouds skittered across the sky blocking out the moon and plunging Jack into pitch blackness every now and again. He waited for the moon to reappear and began to shuffle around the bank, straining his eyes and kicking at brittle tufts of grass. Jack felt his hope fading with each minute. With a final sigh and tears in his eyes he began to turn away. As he did so a sudden bright slice of moonlight revealed an object on the ice. He squinted. It was far out, almost in the middle, and looked to be the same size as his book.

Was he seeing things? Was his mind wishing for the book to be there? He hadn't believed for one moment that it would be on the ice. How was that possible?

'Now what?' he said aloud.

The thought of going onto the ice made him stiff with fear. How could he possibly go out there after his experience just hours earlier? But when he thought back to it, had he really seen anything under the ice...? He couldn't have. Even when he explained it to his gran, it had started to seem impossible and he had hesitated about what he had actually seen. He *had* felt a grip on his wrist and *thought* he had seen webbed fingers, but he had been so terrified of drowning... he could have imagined it... and if there was some sort of terrible creature in the lake, how had he ended up out of the water?

He debated for a moment longer, but just looking towards the centre of the lake where the object lay was enough for him to make his decision. He stepped bravely onto the ice. He didn't want to take any more time to think about what he was doing and how stupid he was being.

His movements on the slippery surface were robotic. Jack thought of his remote control T-Rex. It made a brilliant roaring sound, but moved only with disappointing stiff actions. The ice creaked under his feet and as he got further away from the safety of the bank he felt his breath coming in small, short gasps. He was terrified that the ice would be too thin to hold his weight. He needed to think of something positive.

Three years ago his family had gone ice skating. The four of them had visited an outside rink set up just for the Christmas holidays. All he remembered was his dad spending more time sat down on the wet, icy sludge than skating. He thought about his dad's smile and his laughter that came so easily. He remembered being hot from skating round and round, and then taking off the layers his mum had made him put on. It was the best of memories because his dad had been there. Now his family was like a three-legged dog, hobbling along, getting by, but without the ability to run and play like it used to. Not quite whole.

The memory had absorbed him for a moment. When Jack looked up he saw that he was nearly in the centre of the lake and he could see the object a few footsteps away. He slipped his way forward and bent down. It *was* his book!

He grabbed it and held it close to his face. The plastic cover had kept it dry and safe. How it had ended up in the middle of the ice he didn't know, but he didn't care. Now he just wanted to get back to his gran's. As he turned to head back towards the bank, he realised a fog was beginning to form around him. It was thick and swirling and completely obscured the lake edge.

'Brilliant! All I need now is for the scary music to start and I will be totally freaked out. This is terrible! I wish Gran could be more precise with her predictions.' He laughed nervously.

Jack felt the ice move before he heard it. There was a tremor under his feet. He turned quickly and what he saw behind him made his mouth go dry. Slowly a shape emerged from out of the fog. Jack's immediate reaction was to crouch low in the hope the fog would hide him, but the shape moved quickly.

Jack caught a brief glimpse of a small figure in the weak

moonlight, ploughing towards him with purpose. This person seemed to be pulling a sledge. Stopping in front of him, the figure looked into Jack's eyes. Jack slowly stood up, his mouth hanging wide open. The figure was the size of a small child, but Jack knew he was a man by the deep lines and wrinkles carved into his face. He was dressed in a long white fur coat that touched the ice. He wore tiny matching boots and was wearing an enormous hat that covered his forehead and ears. Jack was so astonished he couldn't speak.

'Ah, there you are at last!' said the man, as if they had arranged a meeting in the middle of a frozen lake at midnight.

'Sorry...' Jack was so surprised that he couldn't think of anything else to say.

'We had better move then,' said the man looking down at the ice and lowering his voice, 'before we have any more trouble.'

Jack couldn't see clearly in the intermittent darkness, but he moved a step closer to the little man instinctively.

'I have brought some furs,' the man said and walked to the sledge. He pulled off a dark rich, chocolate brown fur coat, fur trousers, fur hat and fur boots.

'Screpple fur,' the man announced. 'The best you can get. Mind you, the Screpple has to be dead first. Very difficult to take fur from a live Screpple,' he chuckled to himself. 'You will need these.'

Jack just continued to stare at the man and the furs and the sledge.

'Better move,' the man said hastily, looking down at the ice. 'Get changed quickly.'

Jack found himself doing as he was told. There was something about this little man that made him believe he needed to trust him. He quickly found a tree to hide behind, threw off his clothes and almost jumped into the furs, which fitted him perfectly. He put his book safely into the pocket of the trousers. As he sat on the side of the sledge to slip on the boots he felt warmth flow through his cold body, like an electric blanket switched on in a chilly, damp bed. As Jack was putting on the hat the man spoke.

'Leave your clothes. Follow me and stay close. And do not talk above a whisper. Something is waiting for you. It lost you once and it is trying to find you again. I will take you to the ice tunnel and you will find your way from there. We must go. Now!'

The man put the sledge ropes back over his shoulders and began to move. Jack had no idea in which direction they were heading. He was disorientated and confused by the darkness and fog. He had a hundred questions and they all began to tumble from his mouth at once.

'Who are you? What's your name? What's happening here? This is so, so weird, is this some sort of joke? Are you taking me home? What is that thing under the ice? Is it real? I thought I'd imagined it... I think it tried to kill me!' Jack's voice got louder and louder as his questions became more frantic.

The little man stopped abruptly, put a tiny finger to his lips and pointed down at the ice. It was far too dark for Jack to see anything, but he felt the ice shiver right underneath him. At once he knew what it was. He wanted to run, but the little man indicated for him to keep still. Jack was frozen

by fear, his legs so weak he couldn't have run anywhere even if he had tried.

The shivering stopped beneath his feet for a brief moment. Jack was so still he could hear his heart pounding loudly inside his chest. The little man quietly withdrew a small pebble from his coat pocket. With the gentlest of movements he threw it away from them. Jack heard the pebble bouncing and skidding across the slippery surface. He felt the ice move again, but the tremor moved away from them.

'It's nearer than I thought. We must move now,' said the little man. 'We only have a few minutes before it tracks us again. Quickly, quickly!' he whispered urgently. Jack didn't hesitate and strode in behind the little man keeping his mouth shut, glancing down at the ice every few seconds, expecting the worst.

'On a lake this big I'm surprised it could find us so quickly, but this one is exceptionally aware of you. It will keep looking and I don't expect that it will remain under the ice for long. It will follow you wherever it feels your presence. You must beware. It will not hesitate to take you and the gift you have…'

'What are you talking about?' Jack interrupted him in a hoarse whisper. 'What gift? You're really scaring me now. 'Please you need to tell me what's happening?'

The little man looked at Jack as he walked. 'You really are unprepared for this aren't you? You have had no training at all.'

'Prepared for what?' Jack's voice echoed in the misty silence.

'Shush... quietly. We are nearly off the ice. I will tell you more when we get to safety. Just stay very quiet.'

As they walked on the swirling fog was getting thicker, Jack could barely see the little man in front of him. He was about to speak when the man stopped abruptly and put a finger to his lips again. At first Jack saw nothing other than white mist. Then slowly the mist faded and a black yawning hole in the side of a hill was revealed. Jack could not remember seeing this at the lake before. It looked like a huge sewer pipe. As they moved towards the entrance he tried to get a bearing on where he was and the closer they got the more it reminded him of a giant's open mouth. He took tentative tiptoe steps towards the hole, trying hard not to make the ice creak.

When they reached the entrance the little man stopped and turned to Jack. In the fleeting moonlight Jack saw something familiar in the little man's eyes. It reminded him of his gran; the way she would look at him sometimes. It was a kind, gentle look of sympathy.

The little man spoke quietly again, 'Here is where I must leave you.'

Horrified, Jack said, 'What? No... no! You can't leave me. I don't know what's happening!'

'You will find your way,' the little man said cryptically.

'My way? Where? Please, you have to help me. I need to get home. My gran. My mum. They'll be really, really... worried!'

'This *is* your way home. Your mother will not worry, your gran will tell her all she needs to know. Most come to me with full knowledge. Only two have ever come unprepared. But do not worry, my people will guide you. We are the Silva. We cannot make your decisions or complete your tasks, but we can show you the way home.'

'But… what journey? I have no idea what you're talking about or even who you are. This isn't the way home. My home is across the lake. I don't understand.' He suddenly felt very desperate.

The little man continued, 'You must complete the next part of your journey alone. My time to leave has come. I will, however, give you this advice. Something seeks you, but you must not challenge it. You must hide. It knows you and it knows where you are going. It will follow you.' The little man turned to leave, with a sad smile.

'Good luck! You are strong, but you will need to be resourceful and careful. Always think before you move. One final thing… Do not take any diversions however strong the feeling might be. Keep straight and to the path. Take no turnings and no forks. The road you travel must always be straight.'

Jack was mystified. He looked towards the tunnel in utter confusion. As he turned back to ask another question the little man was gone. Jack now stood alone, tearful and very frightened.

But he took a small, uncertain step forward.

Chapter Five

Jack breathed deeply as he walked into the tunnel. He couldn't see anything in front of him, not even his hand in front of his face.

Not a good start, he thought.

He looked back towards the entrance, but it had almost disappeared into the darkness. He could just make out a few wisps of mist caught in a shaft of pale moonlight. He couldn't decide what to do next – he wanted to try to get home, which meant returning to the lake, yet something told him that he wouldn't find anything that resembled his home out there. It was as though the world had changed and he was now in a different time and place. He thought back to what the little man had said: 'This *is* your way home.' That meant through this tunnel. He slowly moved forward, holding out his hands. He waved them frantically back and forth as he shuffled unsteadily into the darkness.

It was just as cold inside the tunnel and he could feel the breath coming out of his mouth in freezing plumes; to make himself feel better he imagined them as all kinds of shapes – little rings, a rabbit, a dog, even a chicken! Suddenly he tripped on something and almost somersaulted through the cold air, he landed with an enormous thump on his elbow.

'Ouch!' he cried out.

As he landed, a spark of light illuminated the area where he fell. The light came from inside the ice. It was like a tubular light switched on above and underneath him. It was so bright that it blinded him momentarily. When his eyes had adjusted he looked both ways along the tunnel and was disappointed to still see darkness. He had an idea – he stood up and jumped into the darkness. The section he jumped into lit up exactly as the other one had. The section he had jumped *from* was now dark again.

Only a little bit lights up at any one time, he thought. *Jumping up and down must activate the light. Once I've jumped to the next bit, the bit behind me goes dark. Very eco-friendly! Now all I have to do is hop my way out of here… great!*

Recalling that he had tripped over something, Jack jumped back into the dark space to investigate what had caused him to fall. Again this part of the tunnel lit up and he saw a small, oval pebble on the floor and picked it up. It was pale blue and glassy smooth. He turned it over in his hand and saw a small mark on one side. It looked like an upside down Y with a hook at the top. It seemed familiar, but Jack wasn't sure why.

How did I trip on something so small? he thought. He put it in his pocket. 'Time to jump,' he said loudly.

And so the jumping began.

As he moved the ice encircled him. It was a clean, crystallised white and being lit from inside gave it an almost heavenly feel. After jumping for a while in his full-length fur coat, boots and hat Jack felt exhausted. He needed to stop.

He removed his hat, stuffed it into his coat pocket with

the pebble, and then slid down the wall to catch his breath.

Without his watch Jack couldn't be sure how long he had been moving, but his stomach was now grumbling, so it must have been some time. He would usually eat every two hours or so. His mum said he was eating her out of house and home, but Gran always said that young boys had hollow legs and that was why they were hungry all the time.

He tried hard not to think about food as he continued. Another ten jumps and then he would stop. On jump number eight he landed with a thud and a much bigger section of the tunnel lit up.

In front of him were four tunnels: two forks to his right and two forks to his left. But no straight passage – that was just a frosty wall of ice. He stared at the wall for a long time. He knew the little man had told him to keep going straight, but what was he to do if there weren't any straight paths? It took him several moments to consider this and opted for the second fork on the right – the one closest to the icy wall. And then he hesitated. Was he making the right decision?

'Stop dawdling and keep moving,' he said loudly to himself, his voice echoing in the freezing chamber.

He jumped into the darkness of the right fork and to his relief the entire tunnel lit up in front of him. The tunnel was an endless tubular cavern of twinkling, white ice. He walked slowly and nervously into it, heading for the never-ending distance. His legs felt wobbly from all the jumping, and as he stopped to give them a shake, he noticed another pebble at his feet. He picked it up. It was exactly the same as the one he had tripped on. He turned it over and the marking was the same upside down Y. He put it in his pocket.

Jack was feeling quite weary and his fingers and nose were beginning to tingle with the cold. He put his hat back on.

Time to rest, he thought.

Then the lights went out!

Jack frantically jumped up and down, but despite his efforts the lights did not come back on. He stood still, almost rooted to the spot. There was something coming up behind him. It was getting very close. Jack recognised the feeling of dread and in a split second began to run.

Don't challenge it, just hide.

He remembered the little man's words as he took off into the darkness.

One hundred metres was always his best event at athletics, but he knew that his stride would slow once he passed the initial acceleration. Luckily the fur coat, far from hindering him, felt like Lycra and the fur boots like the best running spikes he had ever worn. He felt his heart beginning to strain as he stumbled onwards, blind in the velvet darkness.

Something touched his face. The coldness of it shocked him, stinging his face like the prickles he got on his legs when he brushed past stinging nettles. He knew it was an icy webbed hand. Jack quickly pulled out one of the pebbles from his pocket. He turned and hurled it behind him.

There was a terrible ear-piercing shriek that rattled his bones, then the light flashed on again. Blinded, Jack skidded to a halt. Through half-closed lids he looked behind him and saw, with huge relief, that the creature was gone. With a shaking hand he took the remaining pebble from his pocket and looked at it carefully.

How could such a small pebble trip me up and then be used as a weapon against strange, scary monsters? he asked himself.

Despite everything, he smiled. He thought about his gran. He wished he could speak to her now; she would know what to do. He had always liked his gran's talk about her talent and her premonitions, but had never stopped to think about whether he really believed it. She meant everything to him. His mum was Mum, but since his dad had gone it was like she had disappeared into herself. Sometimes he would come home from school and find her sitting in the garden just staring at the trees. His mum had always been a bit stricter than his dad, but now it felt like there was no softness left inside her, he knew she was grieving and she took care of him and his sister as always, but she had forgotten how to laugh or even how to smile sometimes.

He returned the pebble to his pocket and with a surge of determination made his way forward. He somehow knew that the creature – 'the thing' – was not coming back. Not for now at least – there was far too much pain in that shriek for it to come back for more. At least he now had a weapon if he needed it and so, with a little less wobble in his stride, he continued.

At the end of the tunnel Jack stopped to discover that he had come full circle. This didn't surprise him as he had felt the curve in the passage. As he walked back into the cross section he was uncertain what to do next. The little man had told him to continue along the straight path, but there was no straight path, just a wall of ice in front of him.

Maybe if I just stare at it something will happen…

He tried, but nothing happened.

Jack sat down in the centre of the cross-section of tunnels and stared at the ice wall. As he played with the pebble in his pocket he sensed a connection between the little stone and the way home. He took it out and looked at it again, hoping to find a message that said: THIS WAY OUT!

The pebble, shiny and smooth, sat in the palm of his hand. Then, as he stared, it began to spin. Jack was so startled that he almost dropped it onto the cold tunnel floor. He watched as it began to spin faster and its glassy blue colour changed to dark green then to yellow, orange and then to a hot chilli-pepper red. Jack knew what he had to do – with his fist firmly closed Jack approached the ice wall, his arm outstretched. The pebble was spinning like a mad dog chasing its tail, the heat burning his palm. With all his strength he tossed the pebble into the ice wall. With a hiss of steam it disappeared into the ice, melting the wall as it rotated. Jack watched it move horizontally through the wall, leaving behind a small oblong hole. The ice was very thick, but the pebble didn't stop until it finally disappeared from his sight with a pop!

Quickly Jack put his hand inside the hole and began to scoop. The ice was slushy and it moved easily. He scooped some more, noticeably making a dent. Soon the opening was big enough for him to crawl through. He moved like a mole, scooping the ice from in front of him and pushing it through his knees. Jack was soaking wet, but he knew this was the way out – *the straight path*. His arms began to ache, and he stopped, but not for long, he didn't want to be buried alive in a freezing icy grave.

After an exhausting amount of time his hands were completely numb, but with one final scoop he made it to the other side and fell into the darkness beyond.

Breathing in deeply, Jack recognised the strong smell of of a forest, with pine needles and mossy wood scents. He was exhausted, but despite this he moved around in the dark on his hands and knees sweeping and gathering leaves into a small soft mound. Without considering his predicament he put his head down on his newly made bed, closed his eyes and instantly fell asleep.

Chapter Six

*J*ack's dad was passing him a steaming mug of hot chocolate. *They were in a small, blue tent and he was wrapped up in a sleeping bag – as snug as a bug. They were on a winter camp, but he couldn't quite remember where they were. He thought it was Pembrokeshire. There was only one other tent in the field and that belonged to two smiley-faced walkers who were up at dawn (to make the most of the day) and in bed by the time it was dark, which was pretty early.*

His dad was smiling down at him. 'There you go, son. That'll warm you up.'

'Thanks, Dad,' Jack said, taking the mug. 'This is the best trip we've had yet. Mum would have liked it.'

'You're joking.' His dad laughed. 'You know how much she hates the cold. She freezes in the tent in August!' He chuckled again and Jack smiled back at him.

'Dad… Can I ask you something?'

'What's that, son?'

'Do you think we could stay here, not ever go back?'

His dad's face lit up. 'Oh, Jack, if only… but I'd miss your mum and Jojo.'

'What if they came here too?'

'Wouldn't that be great?'

Jack stared at the man whom he loved more than anything,

and whose warmth and happiness always made him feel so safe.
Then the cosy feeling began to disappear. He felt a shiver run down
his back all the way to his toes.

'I'm cold,' he said.

'Mmm, me too,' agreed his dad. 'I'll just go and dig out another
fleece and a warm pair of socks. That'll sort you out.'

'Dad... don't...!' Jack had an unnerving feeling that his dad
wouldn't return. He could hear him in the little zip-up bedroom
singing. It was a tune he was familiar with, but he couldn't quite
make out the words.

Jack opened his eyes. His world tumbled as his brain processed the reality of his situation. He shut his eyes quickly... squeezing them together tightly... hoping to bring the dream back, but it was too late. His dad, like his dream, had disappeared forever. Jack rubbed his wet eyelids. He hadn't cried for his dad in a while, but talking to him and seeing him so clearly broke his heart again. He lay still for a moment, savouring his father's smile and then he heard the tune – the tune his dad had been singing in his dream.

Jack sat up and looked around. In the darkness of the previous night, he hadn't had a chance to see where he had slept. He shuffled his slightly wet bottom in the nest of dead leaves, pine cones and small twigs. The nest was pushed into the cavernous, hollow roots of an enormous oak tree. As it stirred gently above him it looked as if it was waking in the morning light. Looking up he saw a dense green forest canopy, but not dense enough to stop fingers of sunlight touching the ground.

The tune floated on a light breeze towards him. It was

so melodious that Jack closed his eyes again for a moment. He got up and started to move towards the sound, stopping just to see where he had entered the forest, but there was only a barrier of shrubs, bushes and trees where he had emerged the night before. He turned away, resigned to the idea that his only way home was forward. He had a sense the tune was calling him, and although this adventure had been perilous so far, he crossed his fingers in the hope his next encounter would be a warm one.

As he moved through the trees, Jack realised the winter had not reached this forest. All the trees were in full and healthy leaf. Strangely not all the trees were native. There were ancient oaks, ash and horse-chestnut trees, but next to these towered red woods and strong tall palms. Looking around, Jack saw all sorts of things that both amazed and excited him.

He saw the usual leaf and tree debris, but among the leaves on the ground were all kinds of fruits; some of which he had never seen before. There were apples, bananas, lemons, oranges and even coconuts – all seemingly having dropped from the trees that produced them. Jack couldn't believe his eyes. He knew the names of many of the trees, birds and butterflies, and understood that this forest was not like anything in existence. He smiled as he walked, astonished by everything he saw around him. His dad would have loved to have seen this unique and incredible place.

Thinking of his dad, he automatically reached into his pocket for his *Observer* book. He found it safe and was thankful that despite all the running and jumping in the ice tunnel it had not fallen out. He held it in his hand as he looked around. He wanted to make notes, but the tune called him forward and there really was far too much to see, perhaps he would do it later. He returned the book to his pocket.

It was not just the trees that were unusual. Huge gunnera plants and soft lime green ferns were mixed with beautiful wild orchids and waving bluebells. He saw spring flowers and summer blooms, together with autumn and winter fruits and berries. He smelled wild garlic, a smell so reminiscent of the woodland at home that it stung his nostrils, and he wished for his dad even more. He saw bright, colourful plants and flowers that he didn't recognise.

As he walked, butterflies gently flitted from plant to plant, landing and spreading their wings in the soft, filtered daylight. He knew the Meadow Brown, but the blue African Swallowtail belonged on a different continent. Above his head flew tiny brown sparrows and finches, busy in their daily lives and he glimpsed the long yellow tail of a bird he did not know. He tripped over a tree root while straining his neck to see what appeared to be an Osprey, the most magnificent bird of prey. Just one more thing he had never seen before.

'Oh, Dad,' he sighed sadly. 'I wish you were here to see this.'

The tune still continued to call him and then in the air he caught the smell of something wonderful. His stomach moaned as the smell of bacon reached his nose and mouth at the same time.

He declared out loud, 'Oh! That smells *soooo* good.'

With perfect timing he walked into a small circular

36

clearing. Sat in the middle of the circle, with his back to Jack, was a little man. Jack stepped towards him as if caught in a spell.

The man stopped humming his tune and without turning around he spoke, 'Just in time, Jack. The bacon is perfect, not too crispy. Just as you like it. And I've made some hot chocolate for you too. Please come and sit down.' This little man greeted him in the same familiar way as the little man on the lake.

He was sat on a small log. In front of him was an open fire and on this was a huge pan of spitting bacon. There was also another pan of a thick, chocolaty sauce which bubbled and plopped. Jack sat down on a log opposite the little man, but could not take his eyes from the bacon.

'I know it's your favourite. Please have some.' The little man took an enamel plate from a bag near his feet and placed some sizzling bacon onto it. He pulled out a thick doorstop of brown, seeded bread from this bag and placed it on the plate. He passed the plate across the fire to Jack, who took it and closed his eyes. He ate every mouthful without a breath. When he finally opened his eyes the little man gave him a huge mug of chocolate scooped from the saucepan. Jack took it and drank. It was unlike any hot chocolate he had ever drunk before. This was the real thing – hot melted chocolate and real cream!

The little man seemed to know what he was thinking and said, 'The beans are from the cocoa tree. I grind them and then add the cream from the Screpple milk.'

When Jack had eaten six more pieces of bacon, two chunks of bread and drunk another mug of the delicious hot

chocolate, he finally looked at his companion properly for the first time.

The little man, who had been sitting quietly watching him eat, smiled. His wise grey eyes creased so much that they nearly disappeared. He looked a lot like the first man on the lake. However, instead of furs this little man was wearing animal skins, a bit like the suede coat his sister had. He wore a light brown skin jacket, trousers and skin boots, topped off with a little beanie hat.

'I'm sorry for being such a pig,' Jack said at last. 'It's just, I haven't eaten since... well, for ages!' He smiled and hoped he hadn't offended the little man.

'Not at all, not at all, it is good to see a young boy eat so heartily,' the little man said kindly. He sounded just like his gran.

Jack was relieved, 'I couldn't think about anything, but this lovely food. Thank you; it was just what I needed. And it seems that you know my name, but I haven't asked yours.'

'I'm afraid I can't tell you my name,' said the little man quietly. 'It is a name that only those who live in my tribe know.' He smiled apologetically.

'Oh... okay.' Jack was a little hurt and disappointed. He hesitated, 'It's just that I have a million questions...'

'And you will have answers, I promise you, but first I must show you the forest and help you with the next part of your journey. Think of this place as a resting area. Soon you will understand what is to come. For the moment, you will stay with me until the time is right for you to move on.'

'I'm sorry if I'm impatient, it's just everything that's happened so far... it's all been so strange... but I can wait for the answers.' Jack said, feeling a little better.

He changed the subject to something he'd been dying to ask. 'This forest, it's amazing. I've never seen anything like it before. How do all the trees, plants and birds survive together?'

'It is very, very special here, Jack. You will learn much more soon, but I can tell you that this beautiful place is a refuge for trees, plants, animals, birds and even for the tiniest of insects.'

'A refuge?' Jack asked puzzled, 'From what?'

'From extinction in your world,' the little man replied solemnly.

Jack was astonished.

'I will teach you all about the forest, and why and how the creatures live here; but not at this moment. It will take us quite some time.'

'But what about my mum? She'll be worried.' Jack could imagine his mother's anxiety over his disappearance.

'Don't worry. As you have been told, your mother will know all that she needs to know.'

The little man sounded old and wise and, as Jack looked into his face, he saw that he was a very different person to the first little man he had met on the ice.

Jack sighed, knowing that he had no choice but to trust him. 'Would you mind if I called you "Mr Two" then because you are the second of your people to help me?' Jack didn't want to offend, but he *needed* to give him a name.

The little man stared at him for a moment and then began to chuckle.

'Of course, of course,' he said warmly. 'It is not our

tradition to give our names to those outside the Silva people, but you are young and far from home, so for you Mr Two it shall be.'

Jack breathed a sigh of relief. Upsetting the only person who can help you was not something he had really wanted to do!

'Now there are many things to do, Jack, and the first is to change out of those furs. They will be far too warm for the climate in the forest. I have brought you some Screpple skins.'

From his bag Mr Two pulled out an almost identical copy of the clothes he was wearing, but in a bigger size. Jack wondered if the bag was covering a hole in the ground where Mr Two was keeping all the things. Jack hid behind a bush and took off his furs and pulled on the skin jacket, trousers and boots. He even had a little beanie hat like Mr Two. He was very pleased with his look and smiled.

'What do you think?' he asked, turning in a circle.

'A perfect fit, a perfect fit,' Mr Two said, smiling at him. 'Come, come. We must leave now. We have far to travel and much to see along the way.'

'Oh, I almost forgot,' Jack reached into the pocket of the fur trousers and pulled out his book. He put it in the pocket of his new trousers.

Jack watched as Mr Two collected the chocolate pot, greasy saucepan and his discarded furs and put them all inside his little canvas bag. Rather oddly the bag did not seem to get any bigger. Mr Two pulled out a tiny drawstring pouch from his pocket and poured its sandy contents onto the fire. Immediately the fire went out and dispersed itself into a tiny black charcoal heap. Mr Two looked at Jack.

'The charcoal can be used to re-make the fire. Now we can leave.' He looked around. 'Everything neat and tidy. Yes, yes, neat and tidy. Now come along, follow me.'

Jack looked back at the clearing as they made their way into the forest. Everything *was* neat and tidy.

Chapter Seven

Jack followed Mr Two through the thick undergrowth as sunlight sprinkled itself onto everything around them. He was mesmerised by the trees, plants, birds and butterflies and could have sworn he saw a parrot flying high in the tree tops. Now and again he even recognised the sounds of calling crows and rooks.

What a strange and wonderful place, he thought. *Like the Garden of Eden.*

Jack and Mr Two walked for hours, but for Jack this was definitely the best part of his journey so far. His stomach was full and his feet hardly ached at all. As Jack stopped to look at a mighty Baobab tree he lost sight of Mr Two and began to panic. With relief he saw a tiny door carved into the trunk of the giant tree. It was standing open. Jack hurriedly crawled through and found, to his surprise, that the area inside was big – at least as big as his gran's front room and kitchen together. It had no ceiling and Jack found that he could stand up straight. Above him stretched a hollow trunk like a long, dark train tunnel.

Mr Two stood in the centre, 'Welcome, Jack, to my home... to my home. This is where we will live until you are ready to leave,' he said proudly.

Jack looked around. To his left was a small oak kitchen,

its cabinets curving around half the perimeter of the room. Every cupboard was carved intricately with a delicate floral design. Shelves above the work tops were curved and stacked neatly with copper pots and pans and china cups and plates. A little sink sat in the middle of the smooth curved, ash work tops. The bedroom was sectioned off by a small framed partition made with pale gold silk panels. Jack could see two oval beds that lay end to end, with a small bed at the foot of the much larger one. Each bed was covered in soft quilts and topped with chocolate, brown and snowy white furs. Jack felt drowsy just looking at them.

On his right was a small living area, with two round overstuffed and comfortable looking chairs on a round golden, woolly rug. In the centre of the room a magnificent, circular beech wood table took pride of place. It was lower than usual tables, but it could easily have sat ten people around it. The wood shone and the whole room smelled of lemony, beeswax polish. It was a smell that reminded him of his gran's house. Once again, Jack looked up at the endless tunnel inside the tree trunk.

Noticing where Jack was looking, Mr Two said, 'There is a microthin mesh ceiling about one hundred metres above us. It stops any creatures that live in the tree from joining me down here and it allows lots of headroom as you can see. You will hear the creatures in the night, but please don't be afraid. We all share our home together.'

Mr Two pointed to two small doors carved into the trunk, 'Through the first door you will find the bathroom and if you follow me through the second door, I will show you where I cook.'

Jack had to crouch down to crawl through the little back door, but found that when he reached the other side he could stand once again. Mr Two led the way along a walkway covered with dark green moss, bark and leaves. They were outside the tree now, but the walkway gave them shelter. It led to another round room, but this room was constructed from wooden beams and the walls were made from colossal palm leaves. Positioned in the middle was a small fire pit and Jack could feel the heat and smell the smoky, hickory air.

Looking up he saw a small hole in the roof for the smoke to escape. 'This is my cooking room. Welcome, welcome,' Mr Two said, very excited.

'I cook here because any fire inside the tree could be the end of it... and me,' he chuckled quietly.

Jack nodded, *very clever,* he thought.

A long wooden table was covered in all kinds of shiny cooking utensils. There was also a large straw basket, holding lots of root vegetables: carrots, parsnips, potatoes, beetroots, and some bright yellow and red ones, shaped like melons that he didn't recognise. Hanging from wooden beams were little bundles of dried herbs and spices. Jack could smell mint and thyme, and saw small red chilli peppers on long stalks.

'Now, Jack, you must go back inside and have a warm bath. I will prepare us a meal. Then we must sleep. Yes, we must sleep. We have some very busy days ahead of us,' said Mr Two.

Jack still had many questions to ask.

Mr Two sensed this and said, 'Your questions will be

answered soon, but tonight you must eat and rest. There will be plenty of time for questions and answers. Yes, plenty of time.'

Jack walked slowly back into the tree house. He had to admit that he was enormously tired and the thought of a bath and that lovely, soft downy bed was very welcoming.

He crawled through the second door and found a small bathroom. The bath had been filled with hot water and soap suds threatened to spill over the top. Jack didn't know who had prepared this bath, but then there were a lot of things that he didn't know. He stripped out of the new skins and dipped a toe into the soapy water. The bath smelled of mint and lavender, and as he dropped into the warm water tiredness crept over him. Unfortunately the bath had been made for a very small person and Jack's legs hung out of it like two spindly, sparrow legs hanging over the edge of a nest. He did the best he could to wash himself and eventually he was clean, smelling like the minty water. He dried himself with a tiny towel, not far off the size of a flannel, and then got dressed again.

When he entered the main room Mr Two was sat at the big round table, smiling and waiting for him. Two large orange ceramic bowls had been filled with a steaming stew. Jack's tummy roared loudly at the delicious smell as he wondered just how long he had been in the bathroom.

'Come and sit now, Jack. Yes, sit and eat.'

Jack didn't have to be asked twice. He used a small teaspoon to dig his way through a stew made with all the vegetables he had seen outside, combined with a melt-in-your mouth spicy meat. Next to his plate Mr Two had put a doughy bread roll. As soon as Jack had finished his stew he mopped up every last bit up with his roll, until his bowl didn't need washing. Mr Two then put a warm chocolate mousse in front of him, which didn't touch the sides. Afterwards, Jack simply said, 'Thank you.'

Mr Two nodded and said kindly, 'Right, now. Time for bed, time for bed,' and ushered him towards the bedroom.

On the larger bed he found a pair of soft, brushed cotton pyjamas folded neatly on his pillow. He changed into them and crawled wearily into the warmth of the feather quilt.

Mr Two knocked softly on the door before creeping into the room. He hummed a familiar tune as he sat in the corner, watching the shadows. Jack felt safe and his eyes closed quickly.

Chapter Eight

H*is dad was singing…*
"Climb, climb up Silent Mountain, where the breezes blow,
Climb, climb up Silent Mountain, faces all aglow…"
Jack smiled at his dad.

Then his eyes snapped open. He was laying on his stomach, his head buried in a soft feather pillow, with his arms tucked under it. He moved his head to the side. The world around him was black. He shifted slightly, remembering the soft and comfortable bed. He was still in it, but the warm and cosy feeling had gone. In the darkness he listened, one ear still buried in the pillow. Yet he heard nothing. Fear suddenly prickled his body, moving up from his toes and reaching his brain instantly. He felt like he had woken from a lovely dream into something very real and terrible. He concentrated hard and thought about the tree trunk above him – an empty tunnel of silence. But it wasn't empty. Mr Two had said all sorts of creatures lived up there, but he shouldn't be afraid.

So why was he?

He heard a soft whispering. He waited and then strained to hear it again. It sounded like the rustle of fallen leaves blowing gently on a concrete pavement. The sound seemed to be moving towards him. He was very frightened now: too scared to move his head or even breathe. Should he call out to Mr Two? He listened again. He couldn't hear any sounds from Mr Two. With a huge whoosh of wind, the quilt was torn from his bed and lifted high into the air. Jack remained where he was, startled and terrified, and hugging his face in his pillow. Something icy touched his bare feet.

The need to draw his feet away from the cold was immediate, like pulling his fingers away from a hot candle flame, but he still couldn't move. The coldness began to sting his feet and then pain travelled up towards the back of his knees. It was the same rough stinging sensation that had touched his cheek in the ice tunnel; the same icy fingers that had wrapped around his wrist at the lake. He knew what this was and he questioned how on earth this could be possible.

Mr Two had promised him safety and answers. So how had this 'thing' found him here?

As he lay in silence he felt a glacial heavy weight push down on the back of his knees. Every muscle in his body was straining to move, but his frightened brain would not let them. His fingers flexed under his pillow and touched something smooth and round. Instantly he knew what it was and without any hesitation he flung himself upwards. He twisted around and threw the pebble at the creature, who he felt certain, was crawling along the bottom of the bed. The pebble hit its target and the same cat-like shriek he'd heard in the ice tunnel echoed all the way up the tree trunk. Then the light came back into the room. Mr Two came running in the sleeping room.

'Oh no!' Mr Two cried in dismay. 'Jack! Are you all right?' Mr Two sounded as scared as Jack felt.

Jack had fallen flat onto his stomach, his face buried in the pillow. He turned his head and saw Mr Two's grey eyes washed with concern. That was all he needed as slowly and self-consciously he began to cry. A small sob started in his chest; he tried to hold on to it, but like a great steam train coming out of a tunnel it built up momentum until the sob became huge gulps, shaking his whole body. He lay face down and cried until eventually the sobbing subsided.

Mr Two smoothed Jack's hair and tried to calm him. He spoke gently and much more calmly, 'Now, now, you mustn't cry, it's gone, it's gone. Oh! I should never have left you, oh dear, oh dear! I am so sorry, I am so sorry!'

Mr Two sounded so sad and despondent that when Jack finally lifted his face from the drenched pillow he looked up and saw tears tracking from his crinkled eyes towards his chin. Jack smiled half-heartedly.

'It's okay, Mr Two. It isn't your fault. That thing is looking for me and it found me again. I should have been more prepared.' Jack's tears came again, 'I thought... I thought I was safe here, at least for a while. I think I was wrong.' He looked up and said in a small fearful voice, 'Do you think it's still up there?'

'Oh no, no, the talisman you threw at it will have frightened it off for now, but we cannot linger.'

Hanging above the bed Jack saw the tattered and torn pieces of the grey micro-mesh ceiling. It hung in jagged edges, like small icicles clinging to the guttering of a house. He imagined the creature crawling down the inside of the trunk and watching him sleep. He felt sick but Mr Two had rallied himself.

'Well, Jack. That is it, you cannot stay another night. You should have been safe and I just do not know how it found you here, but if it comes again it will not wait. It will take you and that will be the end!'

Jack shivered and the icy feeling washed over his body again.

'We have much to do, but we only have a day to do it. We cannot take the risk. No, we cannot take the risk,' Mr Two said hastily. 'Right, you must get dressed at once. Then we will eat. I have much to show you before you leave. Hurry now, hurry!' Mr Two marched quickly from the room.

Jack organised his thoughts and began to think of questions to ask. He had found another pebble under his pillow. Thank goodness, but how had it got there? He knew that he would not get all of the answers, but he was determined to find at least *some*. He got up and dressed quickly. Mr Two came back into the room with two hot bowls of porridge.

'What time is it?' Jack asked.

'It is early morning. I was outside preparing food for us when...' Mr Two looked up and grimaced. The two of them ate the porridge quickly and quietly. The porridge was thick and warm and tasted of honey. Eating it gave Jack back some of his courage. As soon as they had finished Mr Two cleared away their dishes and delved deeply into the back of a cupboard. He retrieved a large roll of tea-coloured parchment, almost as long as he was, tied with a piece of string. He uncurled the paper onto the table. It was a very old map, drawn by hand. Mr Two used four lumps of wood to hold down the curling corners.

'This is a map of my world... where you now are,' Mr Two said. He pointed to a spot where small trees had been drawn. 'This is where we are, the Silva forest.'

He traced his finger along a winding line.

'And this is the journey you must make.'

His finger moved easterly across the old and crumpled paper. He stopped at what was obviously a canyon. There was a small bridge drawn across it. Next to this was a desert with an igloo in the middle. The map stopped there. Symbols were drawn on the igloo, like the symbols Jack had seen on the pebbles. Across the map, written in a language he couldn't read, were small neatly formed words, obviously depicting place names.

'It is not exactly precise. Some of the places are just... guesses. But do not worry about that. The most important thing is that you know the next step. You came into the forest here.' He pointed to the drawing of a tunnel, just to the west of the forest. 'Through the ice tunnel. That is the entrance to this world, but it is not the exit.'

Jack stared at the map.

'Why me, Mr Two? I have no idea why I'm here,' he asked.

'Because you have been given the gift,' Mr Two replied quietly.

'What is the gift?'

Jack remembered that the little man on the lake had said the same thing to him.

'I am afraid I cannot say. You must find that out for yourself. That is the very reason you are here.'

Jack became frustrated again and his voice didn't hide this, 'I don't understand!'

Sensing Jack's frustration, Mr Two said, 'As best I can I will explain, as best I can. You come from generations who have been given the gift. One person from each generation of your family carries this gift.'

Feeling calmer now Jack said, 'You mean, like my gran? She always said she had a talent. Like a gift, but I didn't really take that seriously...'

'No, your grandmother has always been special, but it was much later that it became her responsibility to prepare the gifted for the journey here.'

'But she didn't say anything to me. Not once. She didn't prepare me for this,' Jack said, feeling disappointed in his gran.

Mr Two interrupted him, 'I think that your grandmother was still waiting to tell you. I think she probably thought you weren't ready to take the journey.'

'But she told me about the freeze on the lake,' Jack said.

'Yes, she did, but she also warned you not to go to the lake. Perhaps she did not think you would disobey her.'

Jack looked down feeling guilty.

'It is possible your grandmother felt that you had too much sadness already? She probably did not want to burden you with what was to come.'

Jack understood; since his dad had died he had worn that sadness like a coat.

'So my gran, she sort of… works for you?'

Mr Two smiled at him, 'Yes, yes… if you like. She knows of our existence in this world, though she has never been here.'

'How does she know about this place and how to prepare me?'

'Didn't she tell you often enough Jack? She has a *talent*.'

Jack smiled, 'I thought it was, well… I thought it was just my gran… being my gran. If I'm honest I didn't really believe her,' he said, now feeling very guilty.

Mr Two sighed, 'Oh dear. You have missed so much because your grandmother did not think you were ready. You should have been told about your gift two years ago.'

'That was when my dad died,' Jack said sadly.

Mr Two nodded.

'I'm still not sure what this gift is,' Jack said again.

'It is something you will learn about soon, very soon. But you must complete more of this journey before you do. I am sorry, Jack, but I can say no more because I do not know more.'

Jack sighed heavily. He still felt that he had very few answers.

He hesitated before he asked the next question, 'So what was 'the thing'? What was that creature? In the lake, the tunnel and now here?' He looked around almost expecting it to be behind him.

The smile had gone from Mr Two's face and there was

a tremor in his voice, 'Yes, oh yes. That was a terrible Sleaf,' he said with a sigh. 'The Sleafs were once the gifted like you.'

'Like me? How can they be like me? They're scary, frightening creatures!'

'It is hard to imagine, but that was before they changed,' Mr Two said.

'Are there many of them?' Jack asked, hoping the answer was no.

'More than just one, but exactly how many I do not know. Their numbers have decreased and so has their power. A few still remain and they know who you are, they crave the power you will eventually possess.'

'But... why? I don't have any power. What can they possibly want that I have?' Jack asked.

'They wish to possess the gift that you will eventually have,' Mr Two said sadly. 'When the Sleafs were gifted, many hundreds of years ago, they were good and honourable people, but there was one who became selfish and greedy. Over time he turned the other Sleafs around to his grasping ways. That was when they began to do terrible, terrible things to gain power over others, but more importantly over your world.'

Mr Two stopped talking for a moment and dropped his voice to a whisper.

'You see, the power that the gift will bring is so strong that the Sleafs are desperate to obtain it. It will make them strong and formidable once again. The very nature of the gift is good, but if they ever regain the power it will change and terrible things will happen to Earth.'

Jack was bewildered and frightened at the same time. He really wasn't sure what Mr Two was trying to tell him. The question seemed silly and childish, but he asked it again.

'Why me? I might not want to go on this journey or face stupid Sleafs or whatever they're called?'

'You have no choice, Jack. You *must* complete the journey. What you do when you get to the end is up to you. There is no way back for you now.'

'What if I just stay here with you?' Jack asked hopefully.

Mr Two smiled gently. 'You cannot, Jack. We Silva people only serve as guides. We can help you on your journey so far, but only *you* can complete it.'

'But how... how can I complete anything? I'm just a kid. What if I fail? I'm not even sure what it is I'm supposed to do.'

Mr Two gazed warmly at him.

'You are a strong and resourceful boy and you will have help. Do not give up before you begin. That is not who you are. Soon you will understand everything.'

Jack tried to gather this information together. He felt like a drowning boy, his head breaking the surface for air just before he is dragged down again by the current.

'Do you know who saved me on the lake?' he asked.

'I do not know, Jack. All I know is that we were waiting for you and then you appeared clutching your book. Now we must hurry and prepare to leave, so much needs to be done. I wish I could have taught you about the Silva Forest. There is so much for you to learn here, but it cannot be. Your safety is all that matters now,' Mr Two said sadly.

'I have one last question,' Jack said. 'The pebbles, what are they?' He pointed to the map. 'The little symbols there, they're the same as on the stones. I know the symbol, but I just can't remember from where. Do you know what it means?'

'Ah yes, the stones. Think of them as good luck charms. You must collect all that you come across.'

Well that wasn't much help, Jack thought, but he kept this thought to himself.

There were still many answers he didn't have. He understood he was gifted, but gifted in what he still did not know.

Eating, he thought to himself and smiled. *Yes, I'm gifted at eating.* And despite the enormity of his situation he let out a small laugh.

Mr Two gathered up the big curling parchment, tied the string around it and went back to the cupboard.

'Won't I need that?' Jack asked.

'No, no. As I have said there will be others to guide you. Now hurry, we must leave while it is still light.'

Mr Two disappeared through the little door again and Jack stared at the room around him. He had been looking forward to staying here and learning all about the creatures, birds and trees in the Silva Forest. He looked up and saw the torn mesh hanging from the trunk and shivered. Perhaps moving on was really for the best.

Mr Two scurried back in with a small backpack. He handed it to Jack.

'Everything you need, yes, everything is inside the bag.

Now come, come. We must leave.' Mr Two rushed to the door like a little rabbit being chased by a fox. Jack followed, the backpack thrown over his shoulder.

Outside the air smelled of wood and earth and sunlight glistened brightly through the greenness. He began to follow Mr Two as he had the previous day. The woodland was still beautiful, but Jack felt very different now. He had a strange unease in his chest.

Chapter Nine

They walked for many hours. The canopy above was still thick and the filtered sunlight shone on them as they walked. Just as Jack's feet began to grow weary, he noticed that the trees were thinning out. Jack also spotted smaller saplings growing on the forest floor and little patches of grass, which he knew meant more sunlight was getting through. Eventually and without any warning the forest ended. Jack really wasn't sure what he was expecting, perhaps a big sign saying: THE FOREST ENDS HERE!

It was such a shock to be standing in the warm evening sunlight. Jack closed his eyes for a few seconds. He turned his face to the sun and bathed in the warmth like a small lizard on a rock. He opened his eyes and looked around.

The forest has literally ended, Jack thought. *Like someone has drawn a line and said: "no more trees allowed from this point on".*

The air smelled different too and the colour of the soil under his feet had changed to an ochre red. Jack realised that they were standing on the edge of a cliff. Metres away a huge gorge lay in front of him. It was very deep and very wide – a dark red gash in the landscape. The canyon stretched as far as he could see, in both directions. It was both magnificent and scary at the same time. Mr Two had stopped and was smiling sadly at him.

'This is where I leave you, Jack. From here you must face the next part of your journey alone. We have come a long way. I only wish we could have spent more time together, but for now I wish you well, I wish you well.'

Jack didn't know what to say. Eventually he asked, 'How do I get across?'

'The bridge is there,' Mr Two said pointing to the most rickety wooden suspension bridge Jack had ever seen in his life. He almost gulped out loud.

'Before you leave, Jack, I must tell you. You can turn back at any time on the bridge, but once you reach the centre you will be unable to return.'

Oh great, he thought. *Another cryptic clue!*

But instead he said, 'Thank you, Mr Two. You have been very kind to me. I am really grateful for your advice and your wonderful food. Maybe we will see each other again.'

Mr Two put out his hand and Jack bent down and took it.

'Be safe, Jack, yes be safe.' He let go of Jack's hand, turned and went back into the forest.

Jack felt very much alone again and this made him anxious, just like he was at the mouth of the ice tunnel. He tried to calm himself.

Nothing should surprise you anymore, he thought. *So get on with it.*

He walked slowly towards the bridge.

The bridge hung between the two sides of the enormous gorge, but in order to get to it he had to climb down a rope

ladder that was attached to his side of the cliff. He looked down, but immediately wished he hadn't. At the bottom of the drop, looking like a thin black snake, a river flowed. He looked across to the opposite side. It seemed a very long way. The bridge was made of old and silvered wooden slats with very big gaps of air between each step. A fraying rope was strung to the left and right at about waist height so that at least he had something to hold onto.

He breathed deeply, turned and began to climb down the ladder towards the bridge. The ladder swayed gently with his weight and the sensation made him feel sick. At the bottom of the ladder he reached a narrow ledge where the bridge was attached. He tried to push aside a terrible sense of dread.

The bridge, like the ladder, immediately began to sway with his weight. He felt a trickle of sweat run down his back and seriously considered going no further than the first step. Jack tried to think. He wanted to think happy, safe thoughts, but there was a tight knot in his stomach and he couldn't think of anything except just how high he was.

He had never been good with heights; just looking out of his bedroom window at home gave him that dizzy feeling of vertigo.

Come on, Jack, don't be a coward, he thought, remembering his sister Joley flying on a zip wire when she was just seven. It had been his birthday party at a Treetops Adventure Park and he had chickened out of the zip wire and Joley had taken his place. He smiled at the thought of his little sister screaming and laughing – her dark, curly hair flying behind her as she zoomed all the way to the forest floor.

He took another step, then another and focused on the opposite side of the gorge in the far distance.

I'm not going to look down, he thought.

He held tightly to the side ropes and took step after step. After a while he realised he had been holding his breath and took in deep gulps of air. He glanced behind him and saw that he was about a quarter of the way across. Every part of him wanted to turn around, but this would be the end of his journey and getting home was far too important. His backpack felt heavy and sweat had now completely soaked his back. As he got nearer to the centre of the bridge, the wind began to move it from side to side. It was no longer swaying, it was rocking.

He panicked and looked down. He could see miles and miles of nothing below him and then the thin pencil line of the river. He wanted to be sick, but he bravely kept moving. He tried to concentrate on putting his feet firmly on each slat while not looking through the gaps between them. He used his body to rock to the motion of the swinging bridge. As he moved further out into the centre the wind began to whistle and sing. This made his eyes water and sting, blurring his vision.

That's not a bad thing, he thought.

Then he noticed a red circle painted on a slat a few steps ahead.

The centre? he wondered.

Quickly he looked back and realised that it was the centre of the bridge.

'Good, fifty percent done, only another fifty percent to go. Keep moving,' he said out loud.

He put both his feet on the centre slat and that was when it happened. The rocking suddenly worsened as the bridge began to shake, moving violently from side to side like a tiny ship in a big storm. Jack then heard a sound that compelled him to turn completely around and face the way he had just come. There was a loud CRACK! Followed by an even louder THWANG!

The rope on his left dipped and became slack in his hand. The bridge was slowly unravelling and he could see that one by one, where he had just walked, the slats began to snap and break. He knew that he had very little time, so he turned instantly and ran. Unable to slow down, Jack struggled to look where he was running and twice his foot went through the gaps in the slats, touching nothing but air. He could hear the noise of breaking wood behind him, gathering momentum, chasing him. He tried to hold on to the right hand rope, but that too was hanging down almost to his ankles as the bridge continued to swing. He knew that if the ropes broke completely the bridge would fall into the canyon and he would go with it. Adrenalin rushed to his legs and his heart pounded against his terrified chest. He moved swiftly and the other side of the gorge came closer. With nothing to hold onto he felt like he was racing over air.

Nearly there! he screamed in his mind, but when he was just a metre from the end of the bridge, it broke completely free from the other side. Jack felt himself falling into the void and grabbed wildly at the rope that went flying past him. He caught it and swung with it heavily.

With a body-wrenching thud he hit the side of the cliff.

He closed his eyes and prayed that the rope was still attached to something above him. The sound of shattering wood clattered in his ears.

Nothing happened. He fell no further and, relieved, he opened his eyes. He was still hanging and the rope was still attached somewhere above him. He looked up and saw that the edge of the cliff wasn't far above his head. He tried to pull himself up, but knew he would have to get rid of his backpack to do so. Carefully he slipped the bag from his shoulders and let it drop. He didn't look down. The rope was still swaying and he had to use all of his strength to climb hand over hand and eventually over the top. When he reached the safety of solid ground he just lay there, his body was trembling with shock.

Still on his stomach, he turned and scooted forward and peered over the edge. The bridge hung down like a giant broken ladder against the side of the cliff. Far below he could just make out the dots of debris that had fallen. He knew that if the rope had not stayed attached this side he would have been among that wreckage, broken and shattered.

He sat up quickly and wished that he hadn't because his head began to spin and bright white dots appeared in his eyes. Then all went black as he fainted.

When he opened his eyes he was staring at a navy blue sky, overflowing with millions of silver stars. He pushed himself up onto his elbows and saw the moon, a huge white circle in the midnight darkness. It was beautiful. The moon threw a ghostly, pale glow onto the land in front of him and when he finally stood up he could make out shadows of light and dark across the landscape. He was looking at a desert in the moonlight. It lay stretching before him for miles and miles.

Jack was still in shock, his body was bruised and his arms ached from dragging himself up on the rope. And now it was dark he didn't know what to do. Should he start to walk and hope that he would meet someone to help him? Or should he stay put?

He had to be honest, the very thought of trudging into an unknown landscape, in the dark, sounded like something that someone very stupid would do. But he was also very cold and even though the skins he was wearing stopped him from shivering he knew that walking would warm him up.

I bet Mr Two put my furs in the backpack, he thought miserably.

He wondered what else had been in there, probably food and water. He tried hard not to think of food, but yet again, as if on cue, his stomach growled at him.

'Walk!' he commanded himself as found both his footing and his voice.

Chapter Ten

Once his eyes had adjusted to the silver moonlight Jack didn't feel quite so bad. He was cold, absolutely starving, and was aching quite badly from his fall, but his fear had faded a little. He took slow steps, listening out for sounds that might alert him to danger, but thankfully nothing stirred. The ground under his feet began to change from large rocks, to smaller shingle and then eventually to sand. At one point he stopped and tried to make out shapes or forms, he wasn't sure what it was he was looking for – some sign of life, perhaps? But all he could see were the peaks and troughs of shimmering sand dunes in the white moonlight.

He climbed a very high dune. The back of his legs were aching and tired from the constantly sliding sand. When he reached the top he looked around. The desert spread for miles and even though it was dark, the moon cast enough light for him to see nothing but more rippled dunes. He tried not to become too despondent, but once again the gnawing feeling in his stomach stirred. He sat down and took a breath.

What should he do?

He felt very lonely and extremely sad. Tears came to his eyes and he tried to brush them away. He didn't ask to be here, he just wanted to be home. He wanted to be a normal kid again and play football. He was so confused and scared. It was a bad dream, a terrible nightmare. His dad would have known what to do. His dad would have kept him safe. His dad would have smiled and given him an answer. The more he thought about his dad the heavier his sadness became.

'Why did you leave me, Dad?' he shouted into the cold, empty night. 'Why? Why? Why?' he whispered.

The question went on and on until Jack felt his head was going to explode. He tried to make himself stop, but he just couldn't. Eventually he lay on his side and closed his eyes. The song came again.

"Climb, climb up Silent Mountain, where the breezes blow.
Climb, climb up Silent Mountain, faces all aglow.
Turn, turn, your back on sorrow, reach up for the sky.
Climb, climb up Silent Mountain, you and I. You and I."

He must have drifted off to sleep because when he came around his neck ached from the awkward position he had settled in. His face felt stiff and salty where his tears had dried. He sat up. It was still dark. With an aching and resigned heart he got up and began to move again.

He walked for miles. Up and down the never-ending sand dunes. Up and down, hoping that when he reached the top of the next one he would see something in the distance, some sign of life. He had never ever felt so alone.

The moon had not moved in the sky and he wondered if it would ever get light again. As he walked he saw and heard nothing. There wasn't even a breeze. He just focused on the next dune and then the next one. He had almost given up hope.

He reached the top of a very high dune, his calves were hurting and he threw himself down. It was then that he noticed the landscape in front of him had altered. The sand dropped and dipped away into a huge valley. He couldn't see any more dunes but in the far, far distance he saw a minuscule dot of yellow. He knew it was a campfire and immediately his spirits soared up into the starry sky.

As he hurriedly pushed himself up his hand touched something cold and smooth. It was another pebble. He picked it up and held it to the moonlight; the same familiar symbol was drawn on one side. He put it in his pocket and shivered. Whenever he had come into contact with a stone, he had also come into contact with a Sleaf. He turned around warily, straining his eyes. There was nothing but silence behind him. He looked towards the tiny dot of yellow and quickly rushed down the sand dune in that direction.

Despite his ordeal at the bridge his *Observer* book remained safely inside his pocket. Each time he touched the book it was a reminder that he was heading home. The sand became flat and compact as he had reached the valley floor, which made walking easier and quicker on his aching legs.

As he finally reached his destination he could see that he had been right, it was indeed a campfire, but what he hadn't noticed in the darkness was that it was burning on the edge of a small oasis. Tall palms and shrubs surrounded a pool of water. He couldn't see the water, but he could hear it gently sloshing beyond the trees.

A small green tent was pitched next to the palm trees

and roasting above the campfire was a piece of meat on a spit. He almost dived on it, but remembered his manners and called out.

'Hello… hello… is anyone here?'

Nothing answered him.

'Hello, excuse me? Hello…' he called again.

No sound.

There was an eerie silence and Jack felt fear crawl over his body. What if the company he craved was not what he was expecting? He began to back away, slowly.

'Oh, hello!' a voice exclaimed from the bushes. Jack jumped in fright. Out of the darkness walked a girl.

Chapter Eleven

The girl was about his age, his height and she was holding a large jug. She was wearing skins just like his. When she walked into the firelight, two of the greenest eyes he had ever seen smiled at him. Two dark brown plaits framed her oval face. Jack had the strangest sensation that he had seen her before.

'Hello, Jack. I'm sorry if I made you jump,' said the girl. She turned to the trees behind her. 'I was just getting some water. I didn't hear you.' Jack just stared at her but relief had already flooded over him. 'Hello, Jack?' She waved her hand at him.

Jack came to his senses, 'I'm... s-s-sorry,' he stammered. 'I was expecting... someone else.'

'Oh,' she tilted her head to the side and smiled. 'Who would that be then?'

'I'm not sure, I just wasn't expecting... a... a...'

'Girl.' She smiled again, finishing his sentence.

'No, I didn't... I mean...' Jack felt his tongue twisting in knots and his face turning red. He breathed deeply, trying to gain some composure and trying not to make a fool of himself.

'You just frightened me...' There, he had said it.

'Oh, I'm sorry,' she said, a small frown creasing her

brow. 'Right, let's start again.' She put down the water jug, walked around the fire, stood in front of him and held out her hand.

'Hello, I'm Alice.'

Jack smiled at her this time and shook her hand.

'Jack Jupiter. Nice to meet you, Alice.'

'There, introductions over. You are hungry, I presume?' She pointed to the meat spitting and hissing over the flames.

'Um... yes, starving,' he said trying not to sound too desperate.

'Me too, I've been waiting ages for you to get here. Come on, let's eat before we talk. Would you like some water?' Jack didn't need to be asked twice. He took the jug and gulped it down until he could feel the water sloshing around in his empty stomach.

Alice skilfully removed the meat from the spit and tore it into pieces, then put it on a big plate.

'Dive in,' she said.

They sat on the floor in the firelight and devoured the whole piece of meat together. When they had finished they both drank from the water jug and wiped their greasy fingers and mouths on the sleeves of their jackets.

'Mmm. That bit of chicken was fantastic. Thank you,' Jack said.

'It wasn't chicken,' she said. 'It was Screpple meat. Tastes like chicken though, I think. Although, I've never eaten chicken, but that's what I've been told. Go on then, fire away. I know you've got a thousand questions,' Alice said and smiled at him.

'Okay... it's just that I was expecting a little person... you know a Silva person... and when you came out of the bushes I was a little scared and a bit surprised.'

She spoke quietly, 'The Silva people are the guides into this world, through the ice tunnel, and the guardians of the Silva Forest, although there are some exceptions sometimes. My people usually take over when the gifted have crossed the bridge.'

'So you do this a lot then?' Jack asked.

'Oh no, I'm here just for you.'

Jack thought he saw her face turn a little red, but perhaps it was the light from the fire.

'Me? Why me in particular?' he asked.

'I'm a watcher. Well, I'm *your* watcher.'

'My watcher?' he asked again.

'Yes, I have been specifically assigned to watch over you,' she replied. Jack heard pride in her voice.

'But I thought that was my gran's job?' he asked.

'No, no it was your gran's role to prepare you for the journey. Mine was to watch you until you made the journey. But under the circumstances "they" thought that I should also join you too.'

'What circumstances?' he asked.

'Well, we now know that your gran hadn't prepared you and also... um... the Sleafs...' she said with a grimace.

Jack felt uneasy. 'Who are "they"?' he asked.

'You will learn that in time,' Alice said, not answering his question.

I will have to try again, thought Jack, feeling frustrated.

'Okay, you said you watched me until I made the

journey. What do you mean by that? At home?'

'Yes, at home.'

'For how long?'

'About two years,' she said.

And then it hit him, he *had* seen her before.

It had been his first week at comprehensive school, with hundreds of kids everywhere. He new school was so unlike the small, sheltered world of primary school, and he felt completely lost and very uneasy. He had seen her one day in the yard and had remembered her eyes, the way they smiled. He had smiled at her self-consciously, but she had turned away from him. When he looked again she had disappeared into the throng of new Year 7s. He had forgotten about her after that and got caught up in the whole new school thing – making friends, joining clubs and busy timetables.

'You were at my school, weren't you?' he asked quietly.

She nodded, 'You weren't supposed to notice me, but you did. So I had to make myself disappear, but I was still there, watching.'

'Disappear... what like become invisible?'

Alice laughed out loud. 'No, no one can become invisible! No, disappear... like camouflage.'

'Oh,' Jack said feeling a little disappointed. He liked the idea of being able to be invisible.

'It's like... when something is camouflaged. You know it's there... but you can't see it... like a zebra. Its stripes make it stand out on the African plains but in the African grassland it becomes invisible. Unless it moves or you are looking for it, you can't really see it.'

'So you dressed up like a zebra?' Jack said with a straight face.

Alice was about to reply when she saw his smirk. Then they both began to laugh. Jack realised that it was the first time he had laughed aloud in ages.

'Will you be staying with me from now on?' he asked the question hopefully.

'For this part, at least,' she said brightly. 'Just think of it as an adventure.'

'You can say that again... it's like I've been on a rollercoaster. Only it hasn't stopped yet and I can't get off.'

'Is that a good thing?' she asked.

'I'm not sure,' he replied. 'Some of it has been fun, surprising, astonishing... I can't think of any more adjectives. But some of it has been scary – really scary, like the Sleafs and the bridge falling.'

'The bridge?' she asked.

'Yes, the bridge, I thought you knew. I thought it might have been one of those tests the Silva people were talking about. Mind you, it was a pretty dangerous test.'

'No...' she looked at Jack, the frown across her brow once again.

'The bridge broke... it sort of fell into the canyon,' he said.

'Oh no!' she exclaimed.

'Oh yes! I sort of passed out afterwards.'

'That's why it took you so long to get here! How stupid of me. I should have come to find you. I just thought you were a slow walker.'

He smiled at her, 'Yeah, some watcher you are!' A

huge yawn came from nowhere and contorted his face.

'Jack, I'm sorry, it's so late. The moon is a long moon. That means we won't have proper daylight for another three days. We must get some sleep now. You look exhausted. There's some stuff in the tent. We're going to have to share, I'm afraid.'

Jack smiled again, 'You should be afraid, I snore like mad!'

Alice smiled back at him and he wasn't sure how she had done it, but he felt safe again. The sort of safe he used to feel when he was with his dad. His spirits were lifted and happiness had settled on him again.

'Come on then, get into the tent. I'll sort out the fire.' It was an order and he didn't mind at all.

Jack did as he was told. He took off his boots and stumbled sleepily into the tent. More warm furs covered the inside. He lay there for a while listening to Alice putting out the fire and collecting the plates. Then all was quiet and he drifted away into a deep sleep.

When Jack woke he found himself alone in the tent. His sleep had been filled with dreams of his dad again. They had been walking together in a wood, photographing wild flowers to identify later. Jack had told him about the school football team and the great goal he'd scored. His dad seemed very proud of him, rubbing his head with his arm tightly around his neck, which made Jack laugh.

This dream had filled Jack with joy and he was still smiling when he clambered out of the tent. To his surprise the moon was still high in the sky, but the light had changed to the misty grey that comes just before dawn.

The smell of 'just before daybreak' reached his nostrils, together with the waft of something altogether tastier.

Alice was sat next to a small fire, putting something hot and steaming from a saucepan into two bowls. She turned when she heard him coming and smiled at him.

'Good morning,' she said happily. 'How did you sleep?'

'Mmm, good,' Jack replied.

'You talked a lot in your sleep and you laughed a lot too,' she said and smiled at him.

'Oh,' said Jack, feeling embarrassed.

'It's okay. I thought that they must have been nice dreams.'

'Yes, they were nice dreams.' He changed the subject. 'That smells good.'

'Yes, porridge. I hope you like it. We've got to get moving though, once we've eaten.'

Jack sat down next to her and took the warm bowl and spoon she gave him. He ate with gusto.

'Deeelicious!' he said when he had finished.

She smiled again. 'Good, glad you liked it, though how on earth you could have tasted it, the speed you ate it, I'm not sure!'

Jack smiled back, 'It's what I'm good at, eating food scalding hot and really fast. My mum gets so mad at me, but I can't help it.'

'Let's see if you can help clear the camp as fast. I'll go and wash the dishes at the pool. I know you can put a tent away. I've seen you do it before.'

Jack looked at her quizzically, 'Oh really, when?'

'When you went to the Brecon Beacons with your dad.

I was… I was watching.'

'Oh, so that was you dressed up like a zebra?'

She giggled and together they laughed loudly again.

'Come on, Jack. We've got a long way to go today, we had better get a move on!'

When Alice disappeared to the pool, Jack packed away the tent into its own little bag. He was quite proud of himself and the ease at which he did it. When Alice returned they tidied up the campsite and put all her things inside a backpack. Jack picked up the tent and threw it over his shoulder.

'That backpack, it's like Mr Two's. How does it hold so much stuff?'

'I don't really know,' Alice replied, unhelpfully. 'It just does. When we start school we are given one and then we keep it forever.' She shrugged her shoulders and looked as though the thought had never occurred to her. Then she smiled, 'We call it a deepak.'

Jack wished he'd never asked!

'Right then, all set?' Alice asked.

'Sure am,' Jack said, and he really was. For the first time he was looking forward to the next part of this adventure.

They walked together for many miles and for many hours. The landscape was sandy and flat – not a tree or shrub or bush to be seen. They talked about all the things that had happened to Jack so far. He spoke of the things that made him happy, the things he liked to eat and hot chocolate. He found himself telling Alice about the things that frightened him and the things that made him sad. He spoke about Johnson and Stubbs, the two boys who had made his life so thoroughly miserable.

'They are just cowards,' she said. 'Bullies always are. But if you let them scare you, you will be giving them exactly what they want. Perhaps you should tell someone in school about them.'

Alice reminded him of his sister in a way, particularly how she held herself with a grace and confidence that he would never possess.

Throughout his chattering he realised that Alice said very little about herself. When he asked her about family and friends and school she always moved the subject back to him and he found himself opening up to her again. At times they walked for a mile or two in a friendly silence that Jack found comforting, not uncomfortable. Alice laughed freely and he liked the sound that filled the air. They stopped a couple of times to eat some strange fruit and to drink some water that Alice pulled from her deepak.

The moon was still high in the sky. Alice told him that every three months the moon would last for three days, without the sun ever appearing. The light was still the dusty, pearly grey it had been when he had woken up hours earlier. Eventually the landscape began to change. The flat sand started to become hilly again and small sand dunes grew into bigger ones. Jack's legs became weary and because there was no sun in the sky he had no idea of the time.

'I think we had better make camp once we are over the next dune,' Alice finally said and with relief Jack agreed.

Jack had not anticipated that this would be the largest dune by far. As they reached the top Alice turned to him, smiled, then pointed. Jack looked down and what he saw took his breath away. It was the most incredible sight he had ever seen.

Another flat valley of sand spread for miles in front of him and sitting right in the middle of that valley was an enormous, stone… something. The first thing that came to Jack's mind was a colossal golf ball! Jack almost rubbed his eyes in disbelief. He knew what pyramids looked like and although this wasn't triangular at all, it had the feeling of a pyramid – huge pink coloured blocks of stone were somehow connected together to create a giant igloo. A thrill rushed down his spine. It was magnificent. Even from this distance Jack could feel its presence. In the grey light it didn't appear to be real and the more he stared, the more he thought that it would disappear, like a desert mirage.

'That's where we need to make camp,' Alice was whispering and pointing. 'At the base.'

'You knew this was here?' Jack asked, his voice incredulous.

'Yes, but I've never seen it. It's beautiful, isn't it?'

Jack could not speak. All he could do was nod.

'It's called the Korhoz.'

'Who built it?'

'Its origins are a bit vague. It is said that the people who built it were an ancient civilisation like the Incas and it was built as a monument to the planet, but these are stories passed along by word of mouth, no one is really sure where it came from.'

'Come on,' Jack said, his heart was beating fast and he couldn't wait to get to the valley floor. Something inside him was drawing him to the Korhoz. The feeling was so strong he felt it pounding in his chest.

Chapter Twelve

Jack looked at Alice and smiled. She gave him a reassuring smile back and together they moved in silence towards their destination. It took them several exhausting hours to cross the dry, dusty sand to reach it, but when they finally got there they were overawed. They stood at its base and looked up. Their necks craned backwards as they saw the slope of the curve disappear above them. Jack's tiredness was gone. He wanted to walk around it and start exploring, but Alice wouldn't let him.

'We have to make camp here tonight and we'll do everything in the morning. We need to sleep so that we are rested for tomorrow.'

'Why? What are we doing tomorrow?' Jack asked with a smile.

Alice turned and looked up towards the top of the Korhoz, 'Tomorrow we climb.'

'What? Doesn't it have an entrance?' Jack's jaw dropped.

'Did you see an entrance?' Alice asked.

'Well... No, but I haven't been all the way around it yet,' he said, dying to go and look.

'Well, trust me. It doesn't. The only way in is at the top, which is why we must climb it tomorrow.'

'How? How are we going to climb it?' Jack asked incredulously.

'We will discuss that... tomorrow.' Alice had a stubborn look on her face. Jack decided not to argue. Instead he helped her set up camp, all the while the thoughts of the following day running through his mind, he felt as excited as he used to on Christmas Eve, before his dad had died.

Despite his excitement Jack slept soundly. Nevertheless when he woke his anticipation for the day returned. Clambering out of the tent he saw that Alice was preparing their morning meal. Because of the greyness of the day, Jack had no sense of morning or night. He couldn't place the time of day at all. For all he knew it could be 4am or 4pm – his stomach was his usual guide, but even that wasn't working properly. He touched his bare wrist and thought back to the ordeal on the lake. Momentarily he frowned at the memory of losing his watch. Alice smiled at him and his fear was driven away and excitement returned in its place. Jack sat next to her and helped her spoon porridge into bowls.

'Now today, we are going to climb,' she said brightly.

'Yes I've been thinking about that,' Jack said, 'but unfortunately I'm not Spider-Man. I don't have sticky pads on my hands, so how on earth are we going to climb a completely smooth cylindrical object without suction pads? As far as I can see there are no steps and the stone looks as smooth as if it were built of ice like a real igloo.'

Alice smiled knowingly.

'No, you're joking! Don't tell me you have a set of

suction pads in that deep, deep bag of yours?' Jack said in amazement.

Alice continued to grin at him.

'Alice, this is the most ridiculous place I have ever been to in my life. There are Silva people and Screpples, magic and not magic and evil creatures and not evil creatures—'

'That would be good creatures,' Alice interrupted.

'Yes, I know, but I am beginning to think this is the most incredible dream I have ever had and I am going to wake up at any moment.'

Alice leaned over and pinched him hard on the arm.

'YOWW!' Jack howled.

'Well if you were dreaming you wouldn't have felt that. Would you?'

Jack conceded and smiled, rubbing his arm. 'So, okay when are we going to put on the suction pads? I can't wait,' he said with genuine enthusiasm.

'When we've cleared up breakfast,' Alice said still smiling.

As they sat together on the sandy floor Alice pulled eight suction pads from her bag. Jack felt extremely disappointed. He had expected enormous plastic suction cups he could strap to his knees and hands, but instead Alice handed him plastic pads no bigger than the palm of his hand, just like the ones his mum used to stick things to windows – with a suction that lasted for about five minutes. He was not impressed.

'Don't look so dismayed, Jack,' Alice said. 'Hold out your hands.'

Alice carefully laid the suction pads on his palms.

'Tap them twice and you'll feel a little pulling on your skin.'

Jack did as he was told, but looked a little befuddled.

'I can see you don't believe me. Go on, try and pull them off.'

Jack smiled. 'Sorry to disappoint you, Alice, but this is not going to work.' He looked at his hand and the suction pad had disappeared leaving a bright red, circular spot. He looked at the other hand, the same thing had happened there.

'Now go and press your hand against the stone,' Alice said.

Jack got up and walked to the Korhoz. He pressed his palm against a large stone block and he heard a sucking noise. Then his hand stuck like glue. With his hand still attached to the stone he turned and grinned at Alice.

'Um... so how do I...?'

'When you start to climb the movement and momentum of your body will allow you to let go with one hand and stick with the other.'

'Amazing!' he said, impressed.

'What about my knees?'

'The same principle, but the pads will stick to the knees of your trousers.'

'Amazing!' Jack knew he was quickly running out of vocabulary.

'I know,' Alice said, smiling. She handed him the other two suction pads.

He placed them on each knee of his trousers, tapped

them twice and the suction pads disappeared into the Screpple skins, leaving two blue circles this time.

'Colour co-ordinated. I like it,' Jack joked.

Alice did the same with her pads and together they walked towards the smooth wall of the Korhoz.

'Alice, any ideas what we need to do?' he asked.

'We must get to the top and find a way inside. After that, I have no idea. From now on we will need to help each other,' she smiled hesitantly.

'Do I inspire that much faith in you?' Jack asked.

'It's not that, I just feel really scared,' she replied.

Jack reached out and touched her arm softly. 'My dad used to say that if you brave the unknowable with someone it is only half as scary. Whatever happens next we will do it together.'

'Friends together!' Jack shouted loudly.

'Friends together!' Alice repeated. With that ringing noisily in their ears they put both their hands on the first, pink stone block.

Chapter Thirteen

Climbing the Korhoz was easier than Jack had first thought. The suction pads seemed to work in tune with his movements. Even though his actions felt mechanical at first, he soon managed a smooth and fluid motion that made him feel like Spidey! Alice had told him to climb slowly and steadily, which he did, but he felt like a dog on a lead just dying to be released. Alice climbed alongside him and together they navigated their way up the sheer curving slope towards the top. They climbed for a long time, every now and then stopping to catch their breath. Alice produced a bottle of water from her deepak, but Jack was very reluctant to let go.

'You'll be okay. Just hold on with one hand and your two knees.' Jack did this but he felt very shaky. He had visions of quickly sliding back to the base of the Korhoz and landing in a heap of broken bones at the bottom.

They had been climbing slowly and steadily for a long time when, without fanfare, they realised that they had reached the very top of the dome. With both hands still pressed to the warm stone Jack turned and sat on his bottom. At last he had the pleasure of looking around him. The desert spread for hundreds of miles and he could just make out the peaks of the sand dunes and their wavelike patterns.

There was no vegetation, no oasis, not even a single sparse palm tree.

'Wow, this really is a big desert. If you hadn't been here to help me, Alice, I might never have got out.'

Alice was staring at the incredible view too.

'Doesn't it make you feel small?' she said quietly.

'It sure does.'

Jack realised that they were sat on the very top central stone.

'I suppose this is the way in?' he asked.

Alice nodded, 'Yes, but from here I know about as much as you do.'

'Let's not think about that.' Jack smiled. 'Let's try and get inside this thing.'

'What about the suction pads?' he asked.

Alice passed him the water bottle. 'Just wash your hands and splash a bit of water on your knees. The pads will disappear.'

He did as Alice instructed and sure enough the little red and blue marks washed away with the water. Alice did the same.

He tapped on the huge stone he was sitting on and a hollow echo came back.

'Do you have a hammer in that deepak of yours?'

Alice produced a small stone hammer with a flourish. They slid carefully back a little so they were both off the top stone and Jack began to tap… tap… tap… tap… until they heard crack… crack… crack… and with one almighty WHOOOOOSH the entire top stone caved in.

Sitting back on the edge of what was now a very dark

hole sat a stunned Jack, who suddenly laughed.

'Well I didn't expect that to happen! I thought a trap door would open or something. I hope no one saw me, I think I've destroyed a very ancient piece of architecture.' He continued to laugh, looking around him.

They peered down into the darkness. Alice took a small torch from her pocket and shone it into the hole, but the light wasn't strong enough to reach the bottom – if there was a bottom. Jack felt very uneasy. Whatever had been drawing him forward was no longer present.

'I don't like the idea of climbing down there if I can't see the bottom. What if I run out of rope?' he said anxiously.

'I was thinking the same thing,' Alice agreed.

Jack leaned forward a little further desperately trying to adjust his eyes to the darkness.

Alice warned him, 'Careful you don't fall!'

Jack was leaning so far forward that he almost toppled into the hole. At the same time something fell from his pocket. He thought with dismay that it was his book, but with relief realised that it was the pebble that he had picked up in the desert. He heard the pebble land with a soft thump and instantly the inside of the Korhoz lit up. The floor was about two metres below them.

'Well that looks okay,' Jack said, but he sounded more cheerful than he felt. He felt very unsettled now and the exhilaration he had been feeling when he was climbing had disappeared.

'Come on then, I'll go first,' he said bravely.

He held onto the edge of the hole and dropped down through the top of the Korhoz. Alice closely followed him.

They found themselves in a small room, shaped like a Christmas pudding. The walls were perfectly smooth stone, but there did not appear to be a way in or out of the room, except the way they had just come.

'This doesn't seem right. This seems like an antechamber. We need to find a way in,' Jack said.

They both walked to the walls and began to feel around the dusty pink blocks; soon both were equally as pink and dusty, but despite searching for a long time they could not find anything that looked like an entrance. When their fingertips were sore from poking and scraping at the walls they sat down and looked at each other.

'You don't think this could be it, do you? Maybe I was wrong,' Jack said.

'It can't be,' Alice said. 'We climbed for hours to get to the top. This feels like the porch of a house and we need a doorway to get in.'

'It seems to me that we are at the top and what we are looking for has to be… underneath us!' As Jack said this the little pebble began to dim.

'Oh no, I don't like the idea of being here in the dark,' Alice said.

With a grin, Jack moved the pebble and brushed away some of the dust.

He smiled his biggest smile, 'Look! Underneath the pebble,' he said loudly, brushing and blowing the pink dust away. A small circular stone plinth with a groove for a handhold became visible.

'I was right. We should be going down, not out. Help me with this, Alice.' Together they pulled at the heavy stone.

With a lot of effort it slowly began moving up towards them until a doorway was revealed.

Shining Alice's torch through the opening Jack saw the same symbol that was on the pebble, but this time it was carved into a stone staircase that fell away down into darkness. He took Alice's hand and said in a whisper, 'Let's get this over with then.'

They began to go down the thick stone stairs, enclosed by a solid wall, just like those found in ancient castles. Then the walls stopped, and Jack and Alice found themselves descending spiral stone stairs through the centre of a huge, dark, cavernous chamber. Jack was the first to notice the drawings on the wall.

'Look, Alice,' he whispered. He shone the torch into the darkness. Surrounding them were the most beautifully drawn flowers, trees and birds. They were incredibly colourful and had been drawn with such precision that Jack thought at any moment they would move.

'How did anyone manage to draw those?' Alice said.

Both were dwarfed by the size of the chamber and equally minimised by the size of the incredible paintings and drawings on the walls. Their torch was not strong enough to illuminate every detail, but what they could see left them mesmerised as they continued to climb further down.

'I think I need to stop,' Alice said, sitting down on a stone step. She took a bottle of water from her deepak and gave it to Jack as he sat next to her.

'I think we need to keep moving,' Jack said, his uneasy feeling resurfacing.

Alice jumped up quickly.

'Did you see that?' she whispered.

'What?' Jack asked, hearing the fear in her voice.

'On the wall, down there,' she replied, pointing.

Jack reluctantly turned the light towards the wall. He too almost jumped out of his skin.

Then he realised what it was.

'It's okay, it's another painting.'

Jack showed Alice the painting of a hideous creature. It looked crocodilian with its black eyes and black teeth, creating a malevolent picture as Jack stared at it.

'It's so out of place. The other pictures are so beautiful,' said Alice.

But as Jack followed the beam downwards he could see the walls and the paintings had changed. Dark, black and red pictures began to emerge.

'Come on,' he said quickly to Alice and took her hand. As they descended, the pictures became more and more monstrous. Red-eyed creatures, that Jack could not name, were drawn entangled with snake-like animals and beasts, and monsters with scales and sharp teeth. Everywhere Jack and Alice looked they felt red and black eyes staring at them. The birds, flowers and trees further above had disappeared and had been replaced with evil, vile ugly things that had no names.

Eventually Jack stopped shining the torch at the walls. Clasping Alice's hand tightly he kept the torch on the steps in front of them, but despite doing this he still felt as though the darkness was closing in on them. And with it, the terrible things he had seen on the walls creeping towards them.

*

The steps began to get narrower and after a lifetime of climbing down they finally reached the base of the Korhoz. The darkness spread before them like thick, black treacle and the dank, musty smell hurt their noses. They couldn't see any further than the thin torchlight and that was just more darkness.

'Do you hear that?' asked Alice.

'What?' replied Jack, trying to listen hard. 'I hear it. It sounds like water.'

It *did* sound like water. A gentle drip, drip, drip.

'Come on,' Jack said, much more bravely than he felt. 'Let's see how far we can get.'

'I'm scared,' Alice said. And this was the first time Jack felt as though the weight of this journey was back on his shoulders. Alice had been carrying him forward for so long that he had forgotten what it was like to be fearful and afraid of what was to come.

'Do you have anything we can use for more light in the deepak?' Jack asked.

'I'm not sure, hold on, I'll look.'

Alice delved into her deepak and with a delighted smile pulled out a small matchstick.

'Um, Alice, that's a matchstick. I was thinking more like a bigger torch!'

Alice smiled again, 'No, silly, it's a glow stick. You light the end and it burns like… like twenty light bulbs. I thought I'd left it behind when we camped at the oasis, but obviously I didn't.'

'Do you have any matches to light the… um… match?' Jack asked sceptically, hardly believing that a little stick, no

96

longer than his little finger, could light up like one bulb, never mind twenty!

'No you don't need them you just…' Alice caught the look on Jack's face. 'Jack you have to start believing in me…' She took the small torch from Jack and shone it onto the end of the matchstick. Immediately its tip burst into flames and for a moment Jack had to squint in order for his eyes to adjust to the brightness. The fire died down but the light shining from the tip was twenty times brighter than their little torch. He was amazed and impressed.

'You never stop surprising me,' he said. He grinned at her then held the little match above his head and looked around.

'Oh my!' Alice whispered.

Chapter Fourteen

Jack was stood in the most enormous cavern he had ever seen. The stone steps spiralled up through the centre into the blackness above them. It was so large that even the bright light from the matchstick could not reach the furthest corners. They remained in foreboding darkness. The concave walls were dark pink, smooth and rounded like the outside of the Korhoz. Even more frightening was the lake that spread before them. That sight itself was incredible. It was a huge expanse of still water and was so large Jack and Alice could not make out where the other side lay.

But the thing which really sent shivers down Jack's spine was the colour of the water; it was a deep, dark red looking remarkably and scarily like blood. Alice reached for Jack's hand as they walked slowly to the edge of the lake.

'Sometimes the rocks colour the water. Maybe the dust has turned the water dark pink,' Alice said with very little confidence.

'Well it doesn't look pink to me. It's bright red... like blood,' Jack said fearfully.

'So where do we go from here?' he asked. 'We can't just turn around and go back. I thought this was my destiny.' Jack was feeling very dejected as the fear continued to crawl around inside him. He didn't like the idea of climbing back

back up the steep stairs, past the horrible drawings.

'We need a way across,' Alice said.

Jack looked around, holding the match stick high. They were standing on a small shoreline made of pale pink sand. Behind them were the steps and more pink sand that spread back into the darkness. In front of them were six giant, perfectly smooth and round pale pink boulders lined up along the shore. This wasn't a cave. It smelled earthy and musty like a cave, but there was no driftwood on the shore or cave dwelling plants like moss and lichen. There weren't even any stalagmites or stalactites.

'I think we'll be swimming then!' Jack joked, trying to hide his despair.

Alice looked at him and smiled back half-heartedly.

'No way! I was joking. I've already been in one horrible lake this week, no way and am I going there... no way!' Jack was almost shouting.

'I think it's the only way across. I'm sure we have to get to the other side,' Alice said.

'If there is another side,' Jack said, feeling very alarmed by Alice's suggestion. 'I can swim... I'm a good swimmer, but what if it's miles? Besides, I can't swim *and* use the match stick.'

'We could use these, they're waterproof,' Alice said, holding up two small torches attached to headbands.

No matter what Jack said, Alice had an answer. They stood on the shore for a long time arguing back and forth with Jack giving a negative and Alice responding with a positive. Exhausted Jack finally gave in and slumped to the floor.

'Okay. I'll do it. But this is *not* a good idea. I just feel it.'

'I know, but I think it will be all right,' Alice said

without enthusiasm.

Jack wrapped his *Observer* book tightly in its plastic cover and put it in Alice's deepak after she had assured him that it was waterproof. It was the first time the book had left his pocket since his journey had begun. They attached the torches to her heads and discarded the matchstick.

'This will burn for a little while longer until we are well away from the shore. It will give us some extra light for a bit, at least,' she said as she placed it on the ground.

They dropped into the water reluctantly and slowly, trying not splash any water their mouths. They swam in their Screpple skins and used the deepak as a float. The water was cold, but not as cold as the frozen lake at home. The Screpple skins stuck to Jack's body like a wetsuit.

Somehow the water felt thicker – like they were trying to swim through tomato soup and there was also a terrible tinny smell. Jack was silently praying that they were moving in the right direction, but didn't want to frighten Alice.

They had been swimming for some time when something floated past Jack. It was a dead animal! It looked like a small otter, only its markings were black and red.

'Oh no!' Jack shrieked. 'I knew this was a bad idea.'

Just as he said this Alice cried out. Another larger creature was floating towards them. They stopped and waited, motionless with fear. Thankfully this creature was also dead, but it was much, much larger. It was the same size and shape as a crocodile, but its head was smaller and its snout much longer. Small rows of black teeth were visible on the outside of its snout. Its scales were black and red. Jack could smell its rotting carcass as it came closer.

'We need to move. This is *not* good!' Jack screamed and began to kick fiercely, terrified that something else would come towards them. Only this time it would be alive. He knew immediately what he was seeing – the dreadful creatures that had been drawn on the walls of the Korhoz were here in the lake, only so far they had all been dead.

Within minutes they were surrounded by more and more dead and decaying, frightening monsters. Some were small and rat-like and some were as big as hippos. All were either black or red in colour. They treaded water in the centre of what seemed like hundreds of them. Jack felt as though they were having some magnetic pull on the disgusting things.

'Alice, we have to get out of here, now! Let's turn around!' he shouted.

'No! We have to carry on!' she cried back.

And that was the last thing Jack heard before his wrist was grabbed again by something unknown. He looked around for Alice, but she had disappeared under the water.

He screamed, 'Alice!'

Her head came back up and he realised it was Alice that was holding his wrist.

'Trust me and hold on!' she shouted at him with urgency.

At that moment something tangled around his legs and he tried to kick away from it. Jack knew that they were in terrible danger. He was being pulled under the water by his leg, but he knew Alice had hold of his wrist. He had a vision of himself in some deathly tug of war, where he was the rope that would suddenly be torn into two. He felt Alice pull very hard on his wrist and whatever it was that held onto his leg was suddenly gone.

Jack shook his head violently to remove the water from his eyes. Through blurred vision, he realised he was being dragged in Alice's wake, moving across the water at an enormous speed like a water-skier behind a speedboat. The dead creatures were being pushed aside as soft pink foam bubbled on top of the waves.

How can Alice swim this fast? he thought, realising the impossible speed at which they were now travelling. But like a seal being pursued by a shark, he noticed something dark in the water following them.

He screamed, 'Faster, Alice!' because he knew that this was not a shark, it was far more dangerous than that. The creature was moving almost as fast as they were when Alice shouted something. He didn't hear her because the red water was splashing in his face and ears.

'What?!' he screamed.

'Hold your breath!' shouted Alice.

He had no time to reply, or even to take in a deep breath when suddenly he was submerged under the water still moving at high speed Alice was pulling him along. He opened his eyes, but could see nothing but a dark red murkiness. Alice dived deeper and as she did the water became clearer and the colour more diluted. Jack looked behind them. The creature was right there and in the light of his head torch he was now able to see what it was. Its dark red webbed hands reached out towards him in the water. The Sleaf's face was a hideous mask of grotesqueness. It had long red fangs that hung over its black mouth and two deep, black hollow sockets where its eyes should have been. It was a disgusting sight and

Jack knew he would need to fight with all his strength to escape it.

He kicked his legs as hard as he could but he could now feel the breath beginning to seep from his body. His chest was hurting and his head was feeling light. His consciousness was beginning to leave him and his eyes were closing. He looked ahead, forcing his eyes to stay open. Alice seemed to be clothed in a trillion tiny bubbles. Her legs were beating the water furiously and his last thought was, *how did she move so fast.*

Chapter Fifteen

For the second time he woke shivering. He sat up and looked around. He was still in the cavern, but was now laying on a pink dusty shoreline on the opposite side of the bloody lake. His head and wrist hurt. Alice was sat next to him. He looked down at his Screpple skins. They were drying on his body and were now dyed dark red. Examining his arms, he could see that his skin also had the same ruby tint. Alice sat opposite him looking equally as red wine coloured.

She smiled nervously, 'How are you feeling?'

'Okay... I think... has it gone?' he asked, immediately thinking about the Sleaf.

Alice smiled again, but he could see the crease on her brow had returned. 'I... got rid of it... at least for now.' She looked at the water uneasily.

Looking up Jack saw a tiny light shining from the roof of the cavern.

'I think you have some explaining to do,' Jack said, knowing he was putting Alice on the spot. 'You know what I'm talking about don't you?'

Alice nodded and looked very serious, 'Yes, I know. But you have to understand why some things are best left unsaid.'

'Okay,' Jack said, waiting.

Alice took a deep breath, 'I'm a water baby. I spend as much of my life in water as I do on land. I can breathe in water and I can breathe out of water. I don't have gills or a fish tail, so don't ask! I look like this all the time,' she said looking at herself. 'It's just that I can do both equally well. In my family we are all water-babies. That's it really... My fill name is Alicefior. It means "water".' She looked at Jack, waiting for his reaction.

'Well, I'm not sure that anything can really surprise me anymore,' Jack said smiling kindly at Alice. 'It takes a lot to tell people stuff,' he said. 'How did you get rid of the Sleaf?' he asked looking at the water too.

'You passed out just as we reached the shore. I dragged you out, you're heavier out of water than you are in it by the way, and then it came at us. I used my... um... my spout to hurt it and it dived back in. I think it's still out there waiting for us. But the Sleafs are really cowardly. It takes very little to scare them off. The only problem is they keep coming back. They never give up,' she shivered.

'Your spout?' Jack smiled mischievously.

'I can kind of spit water from my mouth... sort of like a water cannon. But it's not very nice tasting because I use the acid that's inside my stomach,' Alice said with obvious embarrassment.

Jack made a face. 'Oh I see,' he said.

'I don't do it very often. Well it's not the sort of thing you would do. It's disgusting, but it is useful sometimes,' Alice smiled half-heartedly.

Jack began to grin and quite suddenly they were both giggling.

106

Still laughing Alice said, 'This is really serious, we have to get out of here, now. I can't hold it with the water spout for very long. I think that's our way out.' She pointed to the pin hole of light, far above them.

Jack nodded. He looked up at the light coming through a very small hole at the top of the cavern roof, a long way up.

'Suction pads?' he asked.

Alice took the suction pads from her deepak. Quickly they put them on and then they started to climb. Jack looked behind him. He was frightened about being followed again. A thought suddenly occurred to him.

'Alice, were you at the lake... the frozen lake?'

'Yes,' Alice replied, continuing to climb the smooth cavern walls.

'Was it you that saved me from the lake?'

She nodded, 'Yes, I broke through the ice and dragged you onto the shore.'

'Why didn't you say?'

'I thought I'd let you work it out for yourself.'

'Did you do the same thing to get rid of the Sleaf? The spout thing...' he asked.

'I didn't need to. I lost it under the water. I saw it take you from the bank and I sneaked up on it and grabbed you back. Then I just moved as fast as I could and, for whatever reason, we lost it. I put you on the opposite bank and stayed near in case it came back. We were really lucky.'

'Did you put my book on the ice?' he asked, remembering why he had returned to the lake.

'Yes. I had to. It was the only way to get you *here*. After you'd gone I found it on the bank where the Sleaf had grabbed you and I placed it somewhere you would hopefully see it. I'm sorry. I knew how important it was to you,' she said apologetically.

'That's okay,' he replied. 'What you did… that's just so brave. You're so brave, I mean.' Jack was embarrassed. He thought he saw Alice blush, but wasn't really sure because of the tomato-like hue of her skin.

He spoke again quickly, 'But how did you know I was there… at the lake… in the first place?'

'Remember what I said before about always being around, but you not noticing me?'

'Oh,' Jack said, ashamed that she had now saved his life twice.

'Thanks,' he felt himself colour.

'Come on. We have to keep moving,' Alice said, quickly changing the subject.

Jack could feel the blood rushing to his head as they were virtually upside down when they reached the opening. Alice manoeuvred herself through it swiftly. With a quick glance down Jack scrambled up through it too; more than grateful that they didn't have to fight off a Sleaf while hanging upside down on invisible suction pads like two bats in a bell tower.

If Jack had been expecting to be on the outside of the Korhoz when he climbed through the hole, then he would have been very much mistaken.

They found themselves on a narrow, dusty path that was situated at the rocky base of a towering blue mountain; the tip of which was hidden in thick dark clouds. They could see that the pale path wound its way up the side of the mountain, but then it too disappeared into the clouds.

'Silent Mountain,' Alice whispered.

Jack thought he had misheard.

'Sorry, what did you say?' he asked.

'Silent Mountain,' Alice whispered again. 'I thought it was a myth but here it is. Wow! I've heard of it so many times in stories, but I just never knew...' her voice trailed off.

'Wait a minute... no... Silent Mountain? It's just a song... a song my dad used to sing to me when I was small.' His head felt a little strange and he sat down.

Alice looked at Jack, 'Silent Mountain is like... like the end of the rainbow. You hear stories about it and you hope that you cans see it one day, but you sort of imagine it doesn't exist. Do you understand?'

'Yes... but it's just a song,' Jack said meekly.

'It's where we have to go. To the very top,' Alice said in a matter-of-fact way. 'We'll eat first though,' she passed him a bottle of water. 'Here, wash the suction pads off. I think we'll be using our legs from now on.'

Jack took the water and washed the pads off his hands and knees. He couldn't speak and could only watch as Alice prepared the food. He just sat and looked up disbelievingly at Silent Mountain, feeling small and ant-like against its towering beauty.

Jack was dazed. Silent Mountain was the very first song he'd been taught by his dad before he'd even understood the words. The song was almost as important to him as his book. Had his dad taught him the song for a reason? Could this be where this entire adventure had been leading? Was there a message waiting for him when he got to the top? He stared up into the clouds wishing he knew the answers.

"Climb, climb up Silent Mountain, where the breezes blow.
Climb, climb up Silent Mountain, faces all aglow.
Turn, turn your back on sorrow, reach up for the sky.
Climb, climb up Silent Mountain, you and I. You and I."

'What is it you were trying to tell me, Dad?' he whispered.

After they had eaten a bowl of honey porridge they set off.

'Do you think this colour will wear off?' Jack asked absently, looking at his deep pink arms.

'I hope so,' Alice replied.

But Jack was already lost in his thoughts; he was trying hard not to think about where they were actually going. His dad's song repeating over and over in his mind.

Chapter Sixteen

There were no trees and no birdsong. Jack and Alice walked quietly together, but Jack's head was full to bursting with the revelation that he was walking the path to the top of Silent Mountain. He dared not believe the one thought that kept coming into his mind. The hope he pushed out each time it reappeared.

He had retrieved his book from Alice's deepak, and now tapped his pocket and felt it safely back inside. He had carried the book throughout this journey, but had only taken it out once, back in the Silva Forest. His dad had told him to take it with him everywhere, but no one could have predicted that it would end up on such a strange adventure. His heart felt heavy as he thought about this.

The incline became steeper as they struggled to put one foot in front of the next. Then the trail became a thin line with vertical, sloping sides disappearing down into the clouds. They had to walk in single file with Alice leading. Jack had no idea how long the climb would take, although he was becoming exhausted. Eventually he called to Alice who was a little ahead of him.

'I think I have to stop. I need to rest.' He felt quite desperate.

It was not just that his energy was sapped. He was also

very concerned about what was coming ahead. The silence felt like it was pushing down on him. It made him feel heavy and lethargic. The hike so far had been frighteningly eerie.

'Look, it widens up in front,' Alice pointed. 'Let's stop there. We can rest and sleep for a little while at least,' her voice sounded too loud in the empty air.

Jack dragged his weary body and tired feet a little further. The path did indeed widen and there was room to put out some furs on the floor that they took from Alice's deepak. They lay down and wrapped themselves up and despite all the dangers that seemed to lurk around them they both fell into a deep sleep.

Jack was woken by something smooth and wet against his ear. For a horrible moment he thought it was the sticky tongue of a Sleaf. His eyes shot open and met those of an animal; he was not staring at a Sleaf but at a camel. He sat up quickly, startled! The camel looked at him and seemed to smile. It stood tall and high above him, its soft white fur curling around its body and back. Jack could see that it had two humps and a long white, curling tail. It had large, blue eyes and a soft, white muzzle and its mouth was open in a permanent smile. Its legs were not long and spindly with knobbly knees, they actually looked more like strong thick elephant legs, covered in the same soft white, curly fur.

Jack smiled and wiped his cheek.

A camel on elephant legs. How strange, he thought.

Alice stirred next to him and opened her eyes, as soon as she saw the camel she too sat up straight.

'Oh, I had no idea that Screpples came this high up!' she

exclaimed.

And then it made sense to Jack. It wasn't a camel it was a Screpple! The creature he had heard so much about.

'This is good,' Alice said.

'How so?' Jack asked quietly out of the side of his mouth. He didn't want to be trampled by a Screpple.

'We can ride it to the top,' Alice replied.

'Are you serious? Are they used to people riding them?' Jack asked sceptically.

'Well, yes you can ride them. It's just um… difficult to catch them,' Alice answered.

'Okay. Do they bite? Camels do and it looks a lot like a camel to me,' Jack asked, still eye to eye with the snowy, white Screpple that had yet to move.

'Sometimes,' Alice replied.

Bravely Jack reached out to touch the soft muzzle that was a few inches from his face. The Screpple didn't flinch. It remained looking at Jack with its lopsided smile. It allowed Jack to rub its nose and it took a small step forward towards him. Jack stood up slowly and whispered gently to the Screpple.

Alice was amazed. She had been a little economical with the truth, as she knew full well that Screpples were often nasty creatures that bit and kicked if you tried to catch them – even though they could be ridden easily once they had been caught, the trick was catching them! She watched Jack smooth, pat and whisper to the Screpple and it didn't make one move to turn and run. He reached its humps, which were a long way above him.

'How do I get on?' he whispered to Alice.

'Pat the front hump. It should sit for you,' Alice replied, her mouth now wide-open in disbelief.

Jack did as Alice said and the Screpple obediently knelt down. He looked at Alice again waiting for further instructions.

'Just pull yourself up,' she said.

And that was what Jack did. Alice stood, grabbed her deepak and moved slowly towards the Screpple, still believing that at any moment it would turn and bolt. Jack reached out for her hand and pulled her up too. There was enough room for her to sit behind him between the two humps. As soon as she was seated the Screpple stood.

'We'll leave the furs and the rest of our stuff here. Anything else we need is in my deepak,' Alice said. 'I can't believe you've done this. Screpple's are notoriously difficult to catch.'

'But you said they were easy.' Jack quickly realised that Alice had been less than truthful. 'Oh, right I see... well perhaps it was my natural charm and it liked the look of me,' Jack chuckled, happy to have done something useful.

Alice raised her eyebrows just as the Screpple turned and began to move up the path as if it already knew where they were going.

They travelled through the dark grey light, but Jack couldn't tell if it was day or early evening as they continued to ride up into the clouds. It was the same ghostly, colourless light that they had experienced in the desert and he didn't like it. All that they could see from the Screpple's back were the downward sloping sides on either side of them – the higher they went the thicker the cloud became and shrouded everything around them. They couldn't see further than the Screpple's long neck and head in front of them, and Jack was hoping desperately that they were moving in the right direction. They didn't speak, but Jack was comforted by Alice's arms around his waist as they moved forward and backward on the Screpple's back. Jack's stomach was growling, but for the first time ever he didn't care.

The mountain remained silent, almost as if it was holding its breath and only the sound of the Screpple's footsteps broke the stillness. The higher they went the colder the air became.

After many, many miles of travel in a noiseless world, the path began to level out and they entered a woodland. Jack couldn't tell if it was large or small; it was too misty. He could just make out the shapes of the trees, stood to attention in their misty coats. There was a stagnant feeling to the woodland that truly frightened him. He was relieved when they finally came into a clearing and the Screpple stopped.

There was no mist here, although the woodland around it was still concealed. It was like being inside the smoke-free circle of a smoke ring. They had reached the top of Silent Mountain and right in the centre of the open space stood a small chapel.

'Am I seeing things?' Jack asked Alice, amazed.

'Well, if you see a church with pink windows, then no you aren't,' Alice replied sounding equally astonished.

The Screpple knelt down to the mulchy floor and they climbed from its back. It then stood and ambled back into the woodland without turning around.

The chapel was made of the same pink, stone block as the Korhoz. There were two solid oak, arched church doors facing them and a small steeple on its west side. It had three large pale pink stained glass windows and its roof was grey slate.

'Do you think I should go inside?' he asked Alice.

Alice nodded.

He walked towards the chapel then realised that Alice wasn't following him.

'Are you coming?'

But he already knew the answer.

Alice sat down on the earthy floor, shaking her head, 'I think this is your part now. I'll wait here for you,' she said, smiling kindly at him.

'Okay,' Jack replied with an uncertain smile.

He nodded goodbye to Alice and then walked to the dark, imposing doors and pushed them open. He waited for a moment then took a deep breath. His legs were shaking and he couldn't stop his hands from trembling as he stepped inside the chapel.

Chapter Seventeen

He was expecting a traditional church to be laid out in front of him, a nave, pews and altar at the far end, but instead Jack stepped into the familiar smell of old books.

Inside the church was not a church at all. Instead there were rows of high, dark wooden shelves containing hundreds, maybe thousands of books. Once again Jack was astonished. The musty smell of words on paper reached his nose and he smiled. It smelled just like his gran's front room. He saw that the church had been turned into a library or perhaps it had never been a church at all and had always been a place of books.

The sturdy shelves stretched from the stone floor to high up into the roof rafters. He wondered how a book could ever be reached from the top shelf. There weren't any modern books with modern covers on the shelves. Instead he saw cracked, leather-bound books that were obviously very old.

He moved to the first row and curiously reached for a red book. The dust rose into the air as he opened it. On the yellowing page he was surprised to see hand drawn illustrations of beautiful red flowers that looked like poppies and faded words written in a script he didn't know. He turned over the page and saw more sketches of plants drawn in minute detail. He put the book back in its place and began to wander along the aisles. Every now and then he stopped and pulled a book from a shelf. The library, because it no longer felt like a church, was bathed in soft pink light coming from the large stained-glass windows high above him.

Jack ambled up and down the passages created by the shelving, lost in the smell and the wonder of holding very old books that had obviously not been opened for many years. He noticed that all the books he looked at contained information about natural history. There were books on animals, trees, plants, birds, bugs and butterflies – an endless list of the natural world, but he didn't recognise any of them. The books were all handwritten and exquisitely drawn. Jack was amazed at the time and the effort that must have been put into the thousands of books that the library held.

He was unsure how long he had been inside the chapel when he had a sudden sense that he was being watched. The hairs on the back of his neck prickled. He had grown accustomed to this feeling and decided not to ignore it. He looked around at the rows of books and the shelves piled high. He had been so engrossed that he had lost all sense of direction. He turned quickly into another aisle. Jack gasped.

Standing at the end of the row was a person. The air was thick and alive with dust mites and the strange pink light from the windows was not bright enough for Jack to see who it was. The person just stood in the shadow of the high bookshelves at the very far end. Jack's immediate instinct was to turn and run, but his fear and something else rooted him to the ground. He squinted into the gloomy light.

The figure began to walk slowly towards him and with a sudden and overwhelming realisation Jack recognised the person's walk. He did not hesitate. He just charged forward as fast as his legs would take him. The figure began to move quickly towards him too and when they reached each other Jack's feet left the ground as he launched himself into his father's arms.

Jack was aware of himself chanting, 'Dad, Dad, Dad!' over and over again.

Then his dad put him back on the floor, held him at arm's length and looked at him. Jack couldn't describe the feeling that was pumping around his body. His wonderful, wonderful dad was stood in front of him; very real and very much alive. The smile that broke on his face had enough light in it to put the sun into competition.

'Hello, son,' his dad said, smiling back at him.

'Hello, Dad,' Jack replied in a whisper. 'Is this a dream?' Not daring to speak too loudly in case it was a mirage that would soon disappear.

'No son, it's not a dream.'

His dad took his hand. 'Come with me and we'll sit and talk.'

Jack allowed his dad to lead him along the dusty aisles of books until they reached a small wooden door. Jack followed behind, still smiling. His cheeks were wet and salty from his tears.

His dad opened the door and they stepped into a room. Two cosy armchairs sat side by side under a tall standard lamp. The chairs were illuminated by the lamp, but the rest of the room remained in a shadowy darkness. Jack could smell the very familiar smell of books and knew that if he could, he would see more shelves of books residing in this room. His dad sat him in an armchair and then sat down beside him.

'Now, where do I begin?' his dad said looking at him.

'Perhaps the beginning would be a good idea,' Jack said, desperate to hear his father tell a long story that would never end.

'Good idea,' said his dad, smiling at him. 'I know you are clever enough to understand what has been happening to you so far.'

'Well, I know that Gran didn't tell me something really important and then I came here through the ice tunnel without really knowing what I was doing or why. I know that I haven't been prepared one little bit for any of it and if it hadn't been for Alice... well she saved my life... twice. I also know about the Sleafs wanting me dead... but apart from all that... no, I don't know anything! I don't know why or how you are here. I never expected to see you again.'

His dad sighed deeply, 'It has been difficult for you, I know. Your gran worried too much about you. She thought you just weren't ready to be told. I'm sorry but the Sleafs don't want *you* dead. They just want the book. If that means killing you in the process... well, that's how it's always been for the Sleafs. Nothing stands in the way of them getting hold of the book.'

'What book?' Jack asked, surprised.

'The Geminata,' his dad replied.

'Dad, I don't know what you're talking about. I haven't got a Geminata book. I don't even know what a Geminata is!' Jack said loudly.

'You do, Jack. It's the book I gave you on your tenth birthday,' his dad said quietly.

'No, that's my *Observer Book of Birds*, Dad. You remember don't you?' Jack was beginning to worry. His dad was forgetting one of the most important possessions he had ever owned.

'Take it out of your pocket and look at it,' his father said.

Jack did as he was told. He removed the book's plastic cover and opened it. Unexpectedly the room was filled with a bright and glorious light that shone from its pages. The light was so dazzling that Jack jumped back in his chair and almost dropped it.

'Oh! Wow! What is it, Dad?' he asked, his face illuminated by the book's radiance.

'It's the Geminata. It's the book... the gift that you should have been told about, before...'

'You died,' Jack interrupted.

'Yes, son, before I died. Close the book and I will tell you the whole story.' Jack shut the book, but suddenly felt compelled to hold it tightly in his hand.

'When I was eleven, just like you, my father died too. The world really did collapse around me and I felt as though my heart hurt every time I breathed in and out. He had given me a book just like yours when I was ten. It was, in fact, the same book you are now holding in your hand.'

Jack looked at the book, astonished.

'It was the only possession that tied me to my father and after he died I used it whenever I could, recording birds, trees and wild flowers. Then one day my mother, your gran, told me something that changed my life forever. She told me that I would be going on an adventure that would take me to a place I had only heard about in a song and that the adventure would end in a revelation that would change my life. She called me the keeper of the gift and I thought she was completely cuckoo! I thought she was grieving so much for my father that it had made her ill.'

His dad smiled gently and then he continued.

'Well we both know that she wasn't ill or mad, don't we? When I was thirteen, my journey began just like yours through the ice tunnel. I had help from the Silva people and, with much more luck than judgement, I eventually found my way to the top of Silent Mountain and the library here. I was told the same story that you are hearing now from my father. He told me that I was the custodian of the book called the Geminata. The Geminata is passed to us from our father. As young children we don't see it as it truly exists. Instead we see a book about nature, about birds or butterflies or trees. But it is the same book that has been used for hundreds of years and once it is revealed the book becomes something else entirely. The Geminata holds the key to the future of life on Earth and as the keeper of that key it is yours to use and to protect.'

Jack could hardly speak. This revelation was far too big to fully understand. He stared at the small, tatty book that he held in his hands.

'Grandad was a keeper of the book too?' he asked shocked.

'Yes he was, but because he died when I was eleven he wasn't there to share the important things that I needed to know. Your gran has always known about the book. My father told her everything and she had to guide me as best she could when he died. She didn't expect to have to do the same for you. That was something I should have done. I'm so sorry. She was waiting for you to be ready, but you already know that.'

Jack nodded solemnly.

'So does Mum know about the book?' he asked.

'No she doesn't. It will be up to you if you want to tell her. I didn't find the right time and she doesn't have a talent like your gran.' He smiled.

'How do I use the book, Dad?'

'You will learn, in time, how to use it cleverly and safely, but that will come in the future. For now you must understand the importance of The Geminata. Do you remember the project you did at school on the Shrill Carder Bees?' his dad asked.

'Yes, I did it for science week,' Jack replied, remembering how much effort he had put into it.

'What did you find out? Can you remember?'

'I learned that we have to find ways to look after the bees and their habitats. They are a keystone species, which means they are a really important part of life on Earth. If the bees die out they won't pollinate our crops and then they would die. That would leave us without food and without food humans obviously can't survive, so the population on Earth could die.'

'That's right,' his dad continued. 'Well, the Geminata will be your guide to discover and save the other keystone species. Without which the earth will surely die. It will be your guide, to help you stop the extinction of these species.

'For far too long, Jack, we have taken too much from nature and not given anything back in return. It is now up to you as the keeper of the Geminata to change that. The book will help you with the decisions you need to make. It will take you on incredible adventures around the world to places you didn't even know existed. There will be sights that will mystify and amaze you in the same way you have been amazed here.

'The extinction of just *one* of the remaining keystone species will mean the end of the planet and the end of the human race. Time is running out, Jack. It will not be long, we are nearing the end. You must use the Geminata to save the world,' his dad paused, 'not much to ask of a thirteen-year-old boy, is it?

'Some of your decisions will not be easy. There will also be people, Sleafs, who will want to take the Geminata from you. This is because the book is so powerful that it is both the extinction and the survival of mankind itself.

Jack was reeling.

'What will the Sleafs do if they get the book?' he asked, he was very frightened now.

'If the Sleafs possess the Geminata it will give them the power to change entire ecosystems and then terrible things will happen. Animals, birds, trees and plants will become extinct. Extreme weather will wash away entire communities. Small tribes will disappear in the rainforests. More ice will melt at the polar caps. They will hold the world's population in their hands. They want that power more than anything else. They don't care about the earth, they would be happy to see mankind fail and die.

The Geminata is both a terrible and wonderful gift that you have been given, but I can't emphasise strongly enough just how very important it is that you keep it safe.'

Jack could feel himself trembling, the book shaking in his hands.

'Did someone try to take the book from you, Dad? Is that why you died?'

His dad paused, 'Yes, son, the accident happened as a result of my connection to the Geminata and I just wasn't careful enough.'

'Was it the Sleafs?' Jack asked.

'Yes... I was trying to get one away from the house. They come in many disguises. The way you have seen them here is not how you will always see them when you are back at home.'

'How will I know them then?' Jack asked, fidgeting. He was feeling very unsettled by what his dad was now telling him.

'You *will* know them. Your instinct will tell you who they are, but they are deceitful and sly, so you must always be wary, always on your guard for them. That is why they almost found the Geminata on the night I died.'

'But I had it in my room,' Jack was frightened now.

'I know and I had to stop them from finding you and the book.'

'You mean you sacrificed yourself for the Geminata? For me?!' Jack was dismayed.

'No, it wasn't a sacrifice. The only sacrifice I made was that I would never see my beautiful family again, but once you have learned the power of the Geminata then one day perhaps you will understand my reasons.'

'And Grandad died for the book too?' Jack asked, already knowing the response.

'Yes,' his dad replied quietly. 'And like him I'm just sorry that I can't be alongside you to help. That is what should happen when the book is passed on. The previous keeper teaches the new one how to use the book safely. There were so many times when I wished that my father had been with me, but you still have your gran. She will help you like she helped me and I know the type of boy you are, I know how resourceful you can be.' He reached out and ruffled Jack's hair.

Jack had so many other questions.

'The books here in the library, they're books about extinct animals and plants aren't they?'

'Yes,' his dad replied. 'Each time something becomes extinct; a plant, an animal, even a tiny insect, it is noted in a book and stored here. The more books that fill this library, the closer we come to the end of the earth,' his dad said seriously.

'But there are hundreds... thousands of books here, Dad,' Jack stated with horror.

With sadness in his eyes, his dad nodded, 'I know, son, which is why we have the Geminata, but the pace at which the earth and all its creatures are being destroyed is so quick that even the Geminata may fail. There is a shelf in this very room that remains empty, for now, but when the final book is placed on it the earth and its entire population will die. We are not far away from that happening. We have reached a point where the extinction of the keystone species means the end of the world.'

Jack suddenly felt very sad.

His dad continued, 'The Geminata is here to save and protect the keystone species. The earth has lost hundreds of thousands of creatures and plants through extinction, but the keystone species remain the most important. Once they die out... well... the earth is lost forever.'

Jack's eyes darkened, 'And now it's up to me? What if I fail, Dad? What if I can't do this? It's too much!'

'You can do this, Jack. I thought the same as you when I was a child, but you have a love and understanding of nature deep inside you and this is what you were born for. The Geminata is extraordinary. Once you learn how to use the book it will show you the right way.'

The weight on Jack's shoulders pushed him down into the chair. The sudden realisation that his dad had been killed to protect him and the world. This made him want to cry again.

His dad reached out and took his hand, 'This isn't the time for tears, Jack. You must remember everything that I've told you, because after tonight, well...'

'What?' But he knew what was coming.

'This is the only time you will ever see me. I have to go after tonight.'

Jack flung himself at his dad and began to sob, 'No, no, Dad, come back with me. We could do this together... please... I hate it without you, I miss you! We all miss you... please! I can't do this without your help. I can't do anything.'

But he could no longer speak. The sobs wouldn't let him and his head hurt with the terrible pain that his dad was going to leave him again. Two years of sadness and sorrow overwhelmed him and he was crushed in a way that he had not felt since the day the police had come to the door.

He had been in bed filling in his *Observer* book; he had seen a buzzard again for the fifth day in a row. There had been a knock at the door. He had heard his mum open it and then that awful, horrifying sound that carried up to his bedroom which was part scream and part wail, 'No! No! No!'

The rest of his memory was a cotton wool blur of neighbours, friends and his gran. A black funeral, a house full of people and then a home empty of the only person he wanted to see. But Jack had not taken any of it in. The grief was too painful, so he had existed in his own world, shutting out the reality and not wanting the truth to reach him inside that world. Now, here he was, his world was crashing down and all the raw feeling and despair shook him until he could hardly breathe. He felt his dad holding him and comforting him with words and with love and very slowly his crying subsided.

'It's time to go now, Jack. Your tears must stop. You have cried too much. You have to go home and I have to leave. It was a wonderful gift just to see you again. I miss you, more than you will ever know. Be safe and be careful. You won't be on your own, you have Gran, she will help you.'

His dad looked so sad; all Jack could do was nod, but he knew that this really was his final goodbye. He took the book, placed it gently in its plastic covering and put it in his pocket.

He reached for his dad's hand and together they walked back through the door into the dying pink light of the vast library. Once again his dad took him along the dusty aisles of books until Jack became dizzy from the constant turning. He was lost in his thoughts when with a slow realisation he became aware that the library was now completely dark, so much so that he could no longer see his dad's hand holding his. He stopped and felt a tugging on his wrist.

'Dad...' Jack said, his fear growing.

'I'm here, son,' his dad said, but his voice was spoken as though at the entrance of a cave, distant and echoing. Jack looked around him. It was too dark to see any of the high shelves that should have been either side of him. He reached out his free hand knowing that he should be able to touch the shelves, but felt nothing but empty air.

A gulp caught in his throat.

'Dad?' Jack asked again. He strained his puffy eyes trying to find his dad in the gloom.

They had stopped walking now and the grip on his wrist was hurting.

'Jack, you had better pass me the Geminata. I will need to keep it safe until you get home,' his dad said, but there was a tone in his voice that Jack didn't recognise.

'Dad?' Jack said, knowing quite well that it wasn't his father's hand wrapped around his wrist.

Jack breathed in deeply and suddenly out of the darkness a Sleaf appeared, huge and menacing in front of him. Up close its face was a disgusting tangle of ugly bitterness and revulsion. It caught Jack around the neck before he could move and spoke in his father's voice.

'Give me the Geminata, son.' It smiled a vile and spiteful smile that had no warmth.

'Where's my dad?' Jack wheezed angrily.

'He's dead,' the Sleaf replied. Its voice still belonging to his dad, 'I tried to stop that little chat you just had with him, but I was too late. But he's gone now. He should never have been allowed to come back here. Still, I have what I came for so it makes no difference and now you shall be joining him.' The Sleaf laughed loudly, no longer in his dad's voice. The laugh was torment and hate rolled up together in a terrible sound.

Jack felt his life being squeezed away, but he knew that he would not give up the Geminata if he had any breath left to breathe.

'Now give me the book!' the Sleaf hissed at him, inches from his face.

'Never,' he croaked as it squeezed harder on his throat.

As Jack felt his life begin to fade a thought came to him.

You aren't a weak child anymore. Stand up and fight like your dad fought for you. You have a purpose now!

With one difficult draw of breath, Jack pulled back his leg and kicked out as hard as he could. If he had been converting a try on the rugby field the ball would have flown over the posts and out of the stadium. His foot connected with the Sleaf and a second later there was a familiar grating screech. The grip on his throat was released and Jack turned and fled. He ran into the darkness just as he had run before and then as he felt the creature on his heels he saw a light.

The door was open to the little room and the light inside was burning brightly, calling him to it. He reached the door and flew inside. Then he was falling.

He was falling through air that smelled of mulchy woodland and pine needles, the light was too bright for him to open his eyes, and then he hit something hard and solid and the wind was knocked out of him, all went black again as he passed out.

Chapter Eighteen

'Dad?' he called, even before he had opened his eyes. He was laying on the ground in a woodland. He wasn't quite sure why, but he had the strange and comforting sense of being home. He sat up and looked around. He found himself once again on the opposite side of the lake. This time, however, he wasn't dressed in one boot, one glove and soaking wet clothes, but in Screpple skins. He stood up cautiously. The sky was an ominous dark grey and it was snowing lightly. His breath came out of his mouth in waves of misty warmness. The lake was no longer frozen in front of him.

He felt a huge mixture of emotions, but also strangely exhilarated. He gently tapped the book in his pocket.

'Okay, Jack, let's go!' he said loudly, but there was still the fact that if anyone saw him this time, he was dressed like a native North American.

He shrugged, *That's the least of my worries.*

Snowflakes landed gently on his hair and face as he jogged quickly through the woodland. When he got to the road he tucked his chin into his chest and ran to his gran's house. The chimney was smoking and a lamp was on behind drawn curtains in the front room. He rang the bell.

His gran opened the front door wide-eyed and pulled

him quickly inside the warm little house.

'I warned you not to go back to the lake,' she said accusingly, without a greeting. 'I knew it! Your dad came back dressed in the same clothes when he was your age. Oh, Jack, you weren't ready!' she said, dismayed. 'There was so much to tell you. I hadn't prepared you at all. I feel so guilty,' and then she pulled him to her and hugged him so hard he thought he would pass out again. They went into her welcoming front room. The fire was glowing in the grate.

'Gran, it's a long, long story, but one I think you've heard before, at least twice,' he said, smiling knowingly at her.

She nodded and shook her head at the same time.

'What day is it?' How long have I been gone?' he asked.

'You've been gone all day. When I got up this morning my key was gone and your bed was empty. I've been worrying terribly.'

'Wait a minute. How can that be?' Jack interrupted her. 'I've been gone for days... weeks. Forever... Oh, Gran. There's so much to tell you...' but he stopped himself.

'You don't have to tell me anything right now, Jack. I already know much of what you've experienced, from talking to your dad and your grandad. It is all real; everything you have seen and everything you have heard. You truly are the new keeper of the book,' she whispered. 'I will help you as much as I can. I worried so much about your grandad and then your father. He was so young... like you... but they both took their responsibility into their hearts. But it's not the time to tell you now. You will learn about that soon enough. You look tired! Get yourself home, and out of those clothes, before your mum catches sight of you. She rang a while ago and I told her you'd popped to the shops for me. You know how I hate to tell even little white lies.'

Jack was tired. He wanted to get home and crawl into his bed, his mind was whirling. He still had a thousand questions, but most of all he was still aching inside after seeing his dad again.

His gran walked him to the door and, as usual, he passed the familiar picture of his dad and grandad on the wall. His grandad was sat in a striped wooden deckchair and his eight-year-old dad was sat on his lap. It looked like a warm and sunny day on a sandy beach. Both his dad and grandad looked so happy, smiling at his gran who was taking the photo. Jack had passed this photograph a thousand times, but today he stopped and looked at it closely. His grandad had his trousers rolled up and was wearing a very trendy vest. On his grandad's left bicep was a tattoo, a familiar drawing that Jack had seen so many times during his journey to Silent Mountain. It was the same symbol that had been etched on the pebbles which had got him out of so much trouble. He pointed to the tattoo astonished.

'Gran, I've seen that symbol of Grandad's tattoo before, what does it mean?' he asked.

'It's the keeper's birth mark, Jack, it's not a tattoo,' she said wistfully. 'Your dad had one too, but it was under his hair at the nape of his neck, so you probably wouldn't have seen it. Your grandad usually kept his covered. It was far too dangerous to show it. But it was such a lovely warm, sunny day...' His gran smiled and for a moment seemed lost in the memory of that day.

'I haven't got one,' he said feeling disappointed.

'Oh, yes you do. You just haven't found it yet,' his gran smiled cryptically. 'Now go home and sleep, there's a lot to be done.'

She hugged him tightly again then ushered him out into the snowy early evening. 'Be careful and ring me when you get in.'

'I will,' he grinned at her.

He waved cheerily at her, before running and slipping all the way home.

He tapped on the patio door and prayed that his mum wouldn't answer. Luckily his sister opened the door. She stared at his clothes and without giving her a chance to speak he said, 'Don't ask!' then raced up the stairs two at a time.

'Be down in a second!' he called to his mum who he could hear in the kitchen. He ran into his room and flung himself face down on his bed. His head was overflowing with a gazillion thoughts. He was getting changed when the telephone rang. He heard his mum answer and then call his name, 'Jack it's for you. Pick it up, up there.'

Jack picked up the extension in his mum's bedroom.

'Hello.'

'Hello, Jack, I'm just checking that you are all right?'

'Alice?'

'Yes, it's me,' she said and Jack could hear the smile in her voice.

'Where are you?' he asked.

'Not far away, but I just wanted to let you know that

whatever happens from now on I will be there with you.'

'But I thought you were a watcher?' Jack said mischievously.

'Well, yes. But now that you know I'm here, I won't just be watching you, I'll be with you every chance I get and always waiting on the sidelines for you.'

Jack felt warm inside and it blotted out some of the ache he was still feeling.

'I'm glad,' he said with a smile.

'Me too,' Alice said back. 'I'll be in touch soon, very soon. In the meantime keep that book safe... and yourself,' and then she was gone. Jack rushed back to his room and took the book from his pocket. He did not want to open it just yet. Instead he held it to his chest and knew that this was the beginning of something really scary, but important and good at the same time.

His mum called him, 'Jack, did you have your tea at your gran's?'

'No! I was too busy running errands for her,' he shouted down the stairs.

'Oh good, because I've cooked you some anyway.'

'Great,' he said with a smile on his face, 'I'm famished!'

Also by Michelle Briscombe…

THE HOUSE ON MARCH LANE

In 1836, Harriet's papa, a ship's officer on HMS Beagle, returns from a long journey at sea. On his arrival home, Harriet and her friend Lily become involved in a dangerous secret with tragic consequences.

Almost two centuries later, Flora's best friend Archie experiences a ghostly encounter at her dad's reclamation and salvage yard.

The haunting takes the two friends on a detective adventure with a difference, and leads them to an unexpected and supernatural discovery.

Flora and Archie & Harriet and Lily's lives are soon entwined in a way that they could never have imagined possible.

THE GHOSTS OF CRAIG GLAS CASTLE

It's flattering when ghosts trust you with their stories – if only they'd stop talking occasionally!

So, when Flora and Archie are offered a trip to Craig Glas Castle in Wales, and a break from talking to ghosts, they can't wait to go. But not everything at the castle is what it seems and soon the best friends embark on another ghostly detective adventure.